BETWEEN WORLDS 1
THE MOVE

LORI WOLF-HEFFNER

ISBN 978-1-989465-31-8 (Paperback Edition)

ISBN 978-1-989465-32-5 (E-book Edition)

ISBN 978-1-989465-33-2 (Large Print Edition)

First and second editions

ISBN 978-0-9950906-6-8 (Paperback Edition)

ISBN 978-0-9950906-7-5 (E-book Edition)

ISBN 978-0-9950906-8-2 (Large Print Edition)

Some characters and events in this book are fictitious. Any similarity to real persons, living or dead, is coincidental and not intended by the author.

Editing by Susan Fish, Heather Wright, Jennifer Dinsmore

Cover design by Fresh Design

Photograph from Adobe Stock

Head in the Ground Publishing

Waterloo, Ontario, Canada

www.headintheground.com

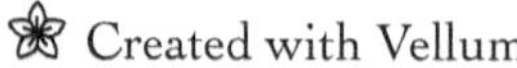 Created with Vellum

This book is dedicated to my grandparents —

John & Mary Heffner
Theresia Heffner
Martin & Magdalena Wolf
Sebastian & Katharina Zimmermann

— who dared to leave everything they knew behind to immigrate to Canada to give their families a better life.

CHAPTER ONE

Juliana opened the door to the second dance studio. Old fluorescent lights flickered on as voices yelled, "Surprise!"

Juliana jumped. The intermediate dance team squeezed through the door and came running at her. Within moments, she was engulfed by friends. As everyone tried to hug her and she tried to hug everyone, Juliana fought back tears, but her friends couldn't.

Miss Kasia, her long black hair pulled into a ponytail, walked up from behind the group. "We've got a little party for you," she said.

Juliana looked up, and only then did she notice that the studio was packed with students, at least sixty or seventy, almost half of the entire dance school.

"Finally!" a five-year-old girl with black pigtails exclaimed. "I've been waiting for hours to hug you!"

Juliana laughed as the girl wrapped her arms around Juliana's hips. Shortly afterwards, all the young kids hugged her in turn on their way through the hall and the tiny change room and into Studio 1. She followed their movements with her gaze and saw that a bunch of different activity stations had been set up.

Miss Kasia smiled as she helped a few parents herd the children. "So you can enjoy some time away from your adoring fans and be with your friends."

Juliana appreciated the gesture, but she didn't mind the young kids either. She was the studio's biggest cheerleader: cheering on the dancers at every competition, helping the younger students practise before they went on stage, and giving novice competitive dancers pep talks while she did their hair. That they'd come to what was clearly a surprise goodbye party for her before she moved halfway across Canada really tugged at her heart. She was going to miss them a lot and wouldn't mind spending a few more minutes with them, even though they could be a handful sometimes.

"Oh my god, Juliana!" Rachel said. "I'm so going to miss you!" Friends since their first class ten years ago, the girls squeezed one another until they could hardly breathe.

Miss Kasia guided the older students back into Studio 2, which was decorated with streamers and balloons in purple and gold, the studio's colours. Messages written in window markers were scrawled across the wall of mirrors.

Juliana wore her emotions on her sleeve—her friends told her that all the time—and tears welled in her eyes. But as the studio's cheerleader, she couldn't cry in front of everyone. Whoever's idea this party was did this to make her happy. She had to stop focusing on the fact that she'd probably never see her home or her friends again: Kitchener, Ontario, was over three thousand kilometres away. Juliana pressed her eyes shut, but that replaced the tears with anger toward her parents. Before that showed on her face, too, Juliana focused her attention back onto the mirrors.

The first panel had messages from her competitive team. As Juliana read them, she forced herself to smile.

I'm going to miss you! Matilda

Remember when you tripped me at Dance Olympia last year? LOL I'll never forget! Linda

You're an awesome partner! Declan

These past few months at the studio had been difficult on Juliana. Because she was moving at Christmas, and competition season started in February, it wouldn't have been fair to her friends if Miss Kasia had choreographed Juliana into this year's comp routines. They would've had to relearn everything in January without her.

Instead, Miss Kasia, being the awesome teacher that she was, gave Juliana the role of dance captain, as though she were in a Broadway musical: Juliana learned the steps and took notes about placement. That way, she could help—and still cheer on her friends!—if someone needed it. Juliana still hated that she couldn't dance *with* them, but her teacher's idea made coping with her impending move just a little easier.

Everyone here knew Juliana so well. How was she going to find friends like this halfway across this massive country?

Juliana walked slowly along the reflective expanse, reading each message on the mirrors and taking as many pictures as she could. One mirror had lots of little-kid-scribbled printing on it.

You teached me how to point my feet! Liliana

Your to tall but I'll still miss you Farah

Youl be famis someday! Jason

With each message Juliana read, she laughed. It took her a little time to read the dozens of messages, and she barely noticed her friends holding up their phones to record it all. If sadness welled up in her throat, she swallowed it.

Declan came up and hugged her.

"You've touched a lot of people. I'm really going to miss you."

"I have the most incredible friends here. I'm going to miss all of you."

Declan moved away, and Juliana leaned toward Rachel. "But I hate surprises."

A coy smile lit up Rachel's face. "Just for once, I

wanted to see how you'd react if something unexpected happened to you."

"This was your idea?" Juliana asked. "You're my best friend!" She playfully punched Rachel in the shoulder and then hugged her again.

No tears so far. Juliana could continue with the brave face so long as the odd joke came along.

"Come over here, Juliana," Miss Kasia said and pointed her toward a plastic chair decorated with purple and gold balloons reaching up toward the ceiling on long, matching ribbons. Juliana glanced over at her mom quickly, and her eyes, too, were a little wet.

Then don't force me to move halfway across the country! she thought in anger.

The young kids were brought back in from their activities, and one by one they handed Juliana a picture they had drawn. It didn't take much effort to realize most of the pictures were of the children with Juliana.

She swallowed her sadness.

"Your eyes are red," said one of the dancers from the pipsqueak classes. Juliana had cheered on their comp numbers whenever possible from the audience. It was something she tried to do for every dance the studio had entered, but especially for the youngest members.

Juliana genuinely smiled at the comment. "I'm just a little tired. But which drawing is yours?" Distraction always worked.

The girl gave Juliana a huge hug. "I'm going to miss you." The girl started crying. "You're a fun teacher."

Except when it didn't.

Juliana sniffled. Now fourteen years old, she'd been allowed to begin the teacher training program this year and had already fallen in love with it. Why did she have to leave all these wonderful people behind?

Juliana walked over to the desk in the studio, where her mom and Kim, Rachel's mom, were standing and talking, and grabbed a tissue to blow her nose with. Mom tried to touch Juliana's shoulder, but she shook off her mother's hand. If it weren't for her and Dad's decision to move, Juliana would be having class right now instead of a goodbye party.

She returned to her seat.

Miss Kasia headed over to the studio computer and clicked a few keys as someone turned off the lights. A video started playing on the white wall opposite the mirrors. The little girl sat herself on Juliana's lap.

Rachel leaned over to her best friend and whispered, "I don't want you to go."

"Neither do I. But Mom and Dad say we're the only ones who can look after my grandfather."

"Don't they have old-age homes in Ontario?"

"Mom says he doesn't have the money for it."

The opening slides in the video showed pictures of Juliana growing up, from her pipsqueak days to her intermediate classes.

"This isn't fair," Rachel said.

"I know. They didn't even ask what I thought about it. Just told me we were moving."

After the video, not a dry eye was to be seen among Juliana's friends. Matilda held up her tap shoes. "One last time?" She was referring to their tap routine, for which they had won a provincial competition last year. Juliana nodded and switched out her hip-hop shoes for her tap shoes.

The entire group, all eleven intermediate tap dancers, took up formation in the studio while everyone else sat along the walls, the little kids in the laps of the big ones.

Miss Kasia smiled at all of them, but held her gaze on Juliana.

"I've known you since you were four," she said. "The look in your eyes is telling me how perfect you want this to be, Juliana. But just have fun. You'll enjoy this—like I tell all of you at every competition—you'll enjoy this more if you have fun instead of worrying about trying to make it perfect."

But Juliana didn't feel an ounce of joy inside her at all. One glance toward her mother and she filled quickly with anger.

The music came on. Juliana, standing sideways, her head bent down and her right hand grabbing the rim of an invisible hat, dropped her heel in time with the beat, a simple rhythm to start the number. Then, one by one, each dancer heel-dropped to their own rhythm, creating a percussion foreground for the music. On a loud cymbal crash, they turned to the front, their heads down, waited eight counts, and then jumped into the opening riff sequence.

As Juliana's feet slammed onto, slid along, and grazed across the floor, she thought of the conversation she'd had with Mom in the car on the way to the studio.

"This isn't fair," Juliana had said.

"I know you're scared—"

"No, I'm not." The last thing Juliana wanted was a heart-to-heart with Mom. "I have my friends here, my dance team, the teacher training program."

"Your new studio also has one."

"But when I emailed them, they said they'd have to see me first and that I'd have to spend at least a year with them before I could be considered."

"You'll need time to adjust to things anyway," Mom said. "If you started teaching at the same time as you started at your new studio and your new school, you'd be too overwhelmed. I know you, sweetheart. If you can't stay on top of things, you fall apart. As it is, we're lucky they accepted videos of your dancing and agreed you can join the competitive program this late in the season."

Lucky? To leave the studio where she had danced since she was four? To leave all these friends?

Now, as the rhythms flowed through her body, her anger grew. She slammed harder and slid farther than usual. Her hands flew into the air on command and stopped, sharp, as though they had hit a wall. She kept looking out the corner of her eyes to stay in line with the others, but the more she looked, the angrier she became. She had travelled to Vancouver and Edmonton with this group, even to Seattle, to compete. They didn't always score high, and sometimes their scores were abysmal, but no matter what happened, Juliana's dance team was always there for her.

She couldn't say the same for her parents, and certainly not about anyone she'd meet in Kitchener.

Cramp roll, cramp roll, da-da de-de, da-da de-de. Prepare, wait, double pirouette, land.

Juliana remembered that time two years before when she'd swung her leg into the high kick that led into the climax of the jazz group, right when the music began its crescendo and the rest of the group had frozen in different positions, waiting for her to land her kick so they could burst into the final counts of the routine. They were at a national championship and had a good shot at diamond, the highest ranking.

But the stage had been too slippery and Juliana had lost her footing, landing on her bum and hands. The fall had shocked her so much that she hadn't been able to move. Normally, the other dancers would have continued dancing around her, finishing the number. And she wouldn't have been angry at them had they done that! But everyone had stopped and immediately rushed to her aid. Miss Kasia had run onstage and conducted a short examination, and doctors had later confirmed her suspicions: Juliana had sprained the ankle of her supporting leg and broken a wrist.

All during her healing and therapy, her friends hung out with her, encouraged her—almost forced her—to come to the studio to watch from the side and to continue learning, and they were there for her when she could finally return to class, her technique weaker. Their frequent texts to keep up her physio, not to push too hard…all of that had kept her going and brought her back stronger than before. Yes, her mother drove her to her appointments, but her father was constantly away at this job. It was her friends who got her through.

Juliana's feet became louder, her arms sharper, her anger channelling itself into the floor. *Flap ball change across, pose, hold for thirty-two…jump up, chaîné-turn in, continue.*

She caught her anger in the mirror, the intensity of her startling even her.

Chaîné-turn out, continue.

Fast flaps, kick, dig, arms, hat.

The music stopped and the room broke out in applause. Mom was clapping, too. Juliana, huffing and puffing, looked around at her fellow dance mates, and everyone's face was wet with tears, not full of anger like hers. They ran together for a massive group hug.

Juliana loved her life in Calgary: she had amazing friends, was in her last year of junior high school, and had just begun learning how to teach dance. Moving now, just before Christmas no less, meant she'd have to leave her friends behind, miss her graduation, and hold off on apprenticing as a dance teacher until at least next year.

The dam that her anger was holding up broke, and Juliana started to cry. Everyone hugged her harder.

How was she going to get through this move to Opa Schuhmacher's without *this* family to cheer *her* on?

CHAPTER TWO

It was November 30, 1919: the first Sunday of Advent and the second Christmas after the end of the war. Each of the four Schuhmacher children scurried out of the house to avoid Mammi's hurry-it-up tap on the bum, and then Tata closed the door behind them.

As everyone stood under the thatch overhang out of the blustery wind, Mammi inspected each child one last time, from oldest to youngest, as she always did: she pulled up the collar on Elisabeth's blouse, tightened Anna's white kerchief, wiped a smudge off Luki's face, and straightened Rosina's apron.

"I will not have my family attending church looking like pigs," Mammi said, and Elisabeth's father gave an approving nod.

Elisabeth tugged at the cuffs on her blouse so they covered her wrists. Although she hadn't grown in a while, some of her clothing just never seemed to fit, and she hated a cold breeze blowing through her sleeves. She slipped her hands into the knitted mittens she'd received last Christmas and pulled her thick shawl tighter over her shoulders. Sometimes she envied the men: their coats looked so warm. However, they were nowhere near as beautiful or as precious as the thick, meticulously embroidered shawls the women wore over their Sunday clothes.

It hadn't snowed in a few days, and the wind had blown much of it off the trees, exposing their grey, dried branches. The ground crunched underneath Elisabeth's feet as the family of six walked down the street to the Lutheran church. Why they had all had to polish their boots, she didn't know.

"One thing I really wanted for Christmas this year was church bells," Tata said.

"What happened to them again?" Rosina asked.

If only Elisabeth could remember so little about life before the war had changed it so much—Rosina was just six. But the war had showed Elisabeth a side of the world she hadn't known existed and wished she could forget.

"Two years ago," Tata said, "the big church bell was taken so it could be melted to make cannons for the war. A year later, the small one, too."

Luki, only eight, and named after their father, chimed

in. "The bells were so loud. I covered my ears whenever we got close!"

The nearer they got to the church, the more families they saw. Elisabeth waved to several of her friends. Her best friend, Maria Haibach, was walking just ahead of them. Maria was a year older than Elisabeth, and her father operated the flour mill in the village. Many of her dresses were made by a seamstress in Semlak, or bought in Arad or Temeswar. She was also already confirmed and therefore looking for a husband.

"Maria!" she shouted, smiling.

"Elisabeth!" Mammi scolded. "No need to look stupid by smiling so much."

Elisabeth tried hard to say nothing; she knew it would only bring her some kind of punishment, especially because it was Advent service they were attending today. But before Elisabeth could close the lid on her anger, her retort escaped her thoughts and flew out her mouth.

"I'm certain Jesus smiled, too," Elisabeth said.

Tata grabbed her wrist and gave her a look of anger that would frighten the devil.

Elisabeth said nothing further, and it wasn't because she was giving in to her father's anger; it was because Tata was leaving for America tomorrow, and she didn't want to quarrel with him on his last day. She would miss him. At fourteen, Elisabeth had already finished her schooling two years ago, and her father had taken it upon himself to continue to teach her. Elisabeth loved nothing more than to sit with Tata after supper, with several gas lamps placed on the kitchen table, and read from the Bible, Martin Luther's teachings, and their family's encyclopedia, which had been left to her Otata, her grandfather, by a family friend a long time ago. She wanted Tata to remember her for how hard she studied, not how quick her mouth was. She took a deep breath, silently asked Jesus for forgiveness, and changed the topic.

"Why can't you find work in Temeswar?" Elisabeth asked Tata. "You could work in a store that has electricity and more customers, and earn more in a day than you would here with farming and shoemaking." Temeswar was a city that lay about ninety kilometres away. Although her father would have to board there during the week, at least he could come home on some weekends.

"Elisabeth," Anna interrupted, "stop asking so many questions. We're almost at church." Only a year older than Luki, Anna attended school with her brother. The teacher had always praised her abilities and she was among the top students in the school, but Anna also knew the unspoken rule: just like everyone else born in the village, her schooling would stop after grade six.

Tata patted his eldest daughter on her kerchief. "I'll miss you, too, Lissika. But I can't earn enough money here. America is the land of milk and honey."

Rosina pushed her way in front of Luki to talk to her

father. "But you're a shoemaker. Don't people in Temeswar wear shoes?"

Tata and Elisabeth laughed.

"Of course they do," Tata answered. "But now that the war is over, our little village and many, many others like Semlak are moving, in a manner of speaking—we are going to become part of Romania. People are scared about that. It means they'll try harder to save money and they won't buy new shoes. After only a year's work in America, I can buy us more land to farm when I return."

"Get out of my way!" Luki shouted at Rosina as he pushed her.

"Mammi!" Rosina cried. "I was just talking to Tata—"

"You were standing in front of me on purpose!"

"Was not!"

"Was too!"

Mammi grabbed both their wrists and dragged each child to either side of her. She then let go and spanked each once. "God is watching," she said.

"We always need to make money," Tata continued, "and farming is always certain: the land here is fertile, and people will always want food. If I could earn money just from making and repairing shoes and save you all so much hard work, I would."

"But why can't we all go?" Rosina asked.

"Why would you want to leave your *heimat*?" Tata asked. "This is where your heart is. Semlak is more than just your home, my sweetheart. It is who you are and where you come from. Your ancestors arrived here a hundred years ago. You know everyone, you can speak with them all, and you can celebrate our festivities with them. When I arrive in America, even though I'll be among friends of friends, it will be different. Very, very different."

Before Elisabeth could say anything, a voice shouted through the crowd of people.

"There you are, Herr and Frau Schuhmacher. We haven't seen you all week! Have you finished packing?"

Elisabeth shuddered. If there was one person in this village she disliked—and may Jesus forgive her—it was Meier Josef. Every Sunday, he moved from one family to the next, asking what was new when he was really trying to learn what was wrong so he could tell others.

Tata shook his hand and Mammi nodded slightly.

"I'm almost done, Herr Meier," Tata said politely. "And thank you for the tip to pack some bread. Lissa kindly baked fresh bread for me yesterday." *Lissa* was what everyone called Elisabeth's mother, whose full name was Elisabeth, too. "My last loaf of fresh bread from her."

"Nobody bakes like a good housewife, I always say," Meier Josef said. Ordinarily, Mammi would nod after such a compliment, but with Meier Josef her head barely moved.

"Do you have the list of names I wrote out for you?" Meier Josef asked.

"It's in my travel bag. I can't thank you enough for it."

Meier Josef tipped his hat. "Then I'll pick you up tomorrow morning at seven."

Tata nodded in acknowledgement before Meier Josef saw another family, waved to them, and headed in their direction. Elisabeth sighed with relief. At the service last week, Meier Josef had wanted to know if Mammi had fully prepared all the food Tata would need, as if suggesting she would neglect her familial duties. It was an impertinent question and Mammi didn't stop complaining about it for the rest of the day.

The Schuhmachers finally reached the church. The yellow-painted, single-steeple structure stood on the east side of the village, like a bright sun in the dead of winter. An Advent wreath adorned each of the two wooden doors of the main entrance. Normally, Elisabeth loved every sight, sound, and smell of Christmas. But this time, she dreaded it: Tata was to leave tomorrow, just as Christmas preparations began.

She wiped her eyes as she entered the church. If Jesus was watching, she didn't want Him seeing her cry.

The children walked up the stairs to sit in the balcony with the other children, Tata split to the left to sit with the other men, and Mammi went to the right to join the women. Omama, Elisabeth's grandmother—and only grandparent—sat at the front with the other older women of the congregation, and Elisabeth could also see many of her parents' siblings, and their older nieces and nephews, sprinkled throughout the church. Maria sat in a special section up front but off to the side for those who were confirmed but unmarried. Elisabeth would join her next spring.

This was one of few situations in her life where Elisabeth truly appreciated all her skirts: where her brother frequently squirmed on the hard pews through the service, and she even occasionally caught Tata shifting around, Elisabeth, her sisters, and their mother could sit relatively comfortably because of the extra cushioning those layers provided.

Light murmurs travelled through their small but packed church as everyone took their seats and greeted their neighbours. They were probably continuing discussions that sounded like the one Tata and Herr Meier had had about their little village soon belonging to Romania instead of Hungary.

The pipe organ silenced the congregation with the opening chords of a hymn, and all stood and began to sing, their voices mixing with the music and filling Elisabeth's soul.

Pastor Fröhlich entered through a side door in the nave, dressed in his black robes. His face stern, his hands folded in prayer, he walked toward the altar like a soldier of Jesus.

Jesus is about to be born, and yet we all look so sad, Elisabeth thought. No one knew what it would mean to belong to Romania, and she didn't know what it would mean to have her father living on the other side of the world.

She pulled out one of the handkerchiefs from her black purse, dried her tears, and wiped her nose.

Why did her father have to move so far away, and at Christmas? She wouldn't hear his voice, or his singing, for at least a year.

CHAPTER THREE

Warm in the ski jacket, toque, mitts, and boots her parents had bought her this year, Juliana brushed snow from one side of the SUV while Dad removed snow from the opposite side. Winnipeg had gotten a good dump last night, which left their vehicle covered in about ten centimetres of snow. Mom was inside the hotel, paying for the room.

Juliana reached the top of the roof with her snow brush and pulled snow in her direction, being sure to get out of the way as it tumbled to the ground.

"This trip would've been more fun in your truck."

Dad had been a transport truck driver all Juliana's life. He'd traversed the Rocky Mountains, travelled to the US, and even occasionally crossed Canada on his routes. When she was younger, she'd joined him on day trips. They ate at truck stops, and she got to blast the horn at stupid drivers.

Compared to the spaciousness and rumbling of a transport truck on the Trans-Canada Highway, sitting cramped in the back seat of the family SUV, with duffle bags piled beside her, while driving through three time zones felt like being trapped in a cage.

Dad hit his snow brush against the tire harder than needed to remove the excess snow. "I've told you time and again that I sold my transport truck because it doesn't make sense to own one when I'd need to build my business from scratch. It took me a long time to do that back home. Plus, your mom and I also figured you'd appreciate this chance to see this magnificent country of ours."

Ugh! It had to be educational, too, didn't it? Juliana thought. She had tried to appreciate the scenery on the drive. She really had. But Saskatchewan was as flat as everyone said it was. She'd taken a picture of a pine and sent it to Rachel, joking that she'd found the prairie province's sole tree. The sunsets and the one night of Northern Lights were more beautiful than the most magical theatre lighting. Juliana would admit that much.

But that fun had totalled an hour. Google Maps said to expect thirty-six hours of driving—assuming no issues—from Calgary to Kitchener. They'd already been on the road for two days, maybe fourteen hours. That was two days trapped in the car with her parents and without any dance to *actually* make her feel better. She also only had quick phone calls over free Wi-Fi to Rachel, not always away from her curious parents' ears.

And they still had another three days to finish driving through Manitoba, then along the northern shore of Lake Superior, and finally *all the way down* into Ontario's arrowhead.

Three…whole…days.

The vehicle cleared, Dad reached for Juliana's snow brush, tapped the brushes against each other, and took them inside the vehicle with him.

Juliana slumped into the back seat.

"I can't believe I have to spend another three days in the car with you." The harshness of her words surprised even her. She mumbled an apology, but it was too late.

Dad slammed his door shut and whipped his head around.

"Sometimes you have to make sacrifices for the people you love," he snapped.

"I don't even know Opa!" Juliana shouted back.

Dad sighed one of those loud "now I'm fed up with you" sighs and turned back to the front. Through the rearview mirror, Juliana could see him roll his eyes in exasperation.

"I saw that," she said.

"Think of it this way," Dad said. "You can avoid cooking for almost a week."

Juliana couldn't stand kitchen work. It involved a lot of tiny actions to create something that would disappear an hour or two later. On the other end of the spectrum was cleaning: once she dusted her bedroom, for example, she could enjoy that cleanliness for the better part of a week. Organize a drawer? Easily several months of satisfaction before it needed another cleaning attack.

Mom got in, passed the receipt to Dad so he could double-check it, stuck it back in her wallet after he okayed it, and buckled up.

"Got your seatbelt on?" she asked Juliana.

"Mm-hmm."

Dad turned on the ignition, and off they drove. After a few moments of silence, Mom clued in to the tense atmosphere in the vehicle.

"What? Teenagers?" she asked Dad.

"Mm-hmm," he replied.

Mom sighed, and Juliana stuck her earbuds in.

Three more days.

JULIANA STARED AT HER PHONE. The restaurant in Thunder Bay, Ontario, had free Wi-Fi, but Rachel wasn't responding to her texts.

Oh, right. She's at her mom's parents. They still make everyone leave their phones in a box.

Juliana sighed. Her parents had cancelled her phone number back in Calgary so she would have a Kitchener number and wouldn't let her hotspot to theirs. Even though they had jobs lined up in Kitchener, her parents wanted to save their data plan while on the road because they said nothing was guaranteed, that things could change before they even started.

Day number three was done, and they were in Ontario, on the northern shore of Lake Superior. The two-hour time difference between Juliana and Rachel made it even more difficult for the best friends to call each other now.

"Jules, have you decided on what you want to eat?" Dad asked.

"What?" Juliana looked up to see the server staring at her with an unnatural grin. Juliana quickly flipped through the menu. "Um…"

"I'll order then," Mom said.

Juliana weighed her food options. Healthy food to support her dancing? Or trucker food that reminded her of those fun days with Dad? Would certainly make her feel better.

Just have fun, Miss Kasia had said, right? By the time the server had come around to Juliana, she'd opted for trucker food: a burger and fries. She handed her menu back.

"Juliana," Mom said, "you know why we're doing this, right?"

So much for fun. "Uh-huh."

"To look after Opa."

"Yup." She scrolled through the photos on her phone, stopping at one of the messages on the mirrors.

"He can't live alone anymore."

"There's always old-age homes." Juliana snapped her head up. It would be nice if she could hide her emotions from time to time. This conversation was pointless, anyway.

Dad shot her a look, and Juliana stared back at her phone.

"This is my father we're talking about. When Oma was in care it was awful, and we couldn't afford something better. I can't do that to him."

Did this conversation have to continue? The move was a done deal. Why waste time talking about it. "Can I look at my photos now?"

"No. I need you to understand. Tata's alone, has early signs of dementia, and never learned how to cook except for boxed cereal, cold-cut sandwiches, and toast. It's just the culture he was raised in. We're worried an accident will happen."

Anger was collecting in Juliana's throat. She looked up. "You have a brother and a sister in Kitchener. They could bring an extra meal. I'm sure they have leftovers like we do all the time. Or when Rachel's grandmother was recovering from surgery last year, their family ordered Meals on Wheels since her grandfather doesn't cook all that much either. I'm sure you could get something like that for Opa. I don't get why we have to move. I won't know anyone."

Juliana knew she was trying her parents' patience, but

they were trying hers, too. With Dad always on the road, often gone for a week or two at a time, and Mom either going in early at the grocery store or staying easily an hour after closing—apparently because that's what managers do—Juliana sometimes had the feeling she was raising herself. What right did they have to tell her what to do? They were hardly home as it was. Rachel's mom probably knew her better.

Mom took a deep breath. In contrast to Dad, who took deep breaths when he was getting angry, Mom took deep breaths when she needed to calm herself. "It's clear you still don't understand everything. Your Uncle Peter's job takes him away from home for weeks at a time, and Aunt Anne has her hands full with six kids."

"Two of them are out of high school, you said!"

Mom pressed her lips into a tight line and took another deep breath before she spoke. "They still live at home and she cooks for them so they can focus on their studies. We didn't make this decision lightly, Juliana. Neither of my siblings can check in on Opa every day. Trust me. I talked to them."

"And not to me."

Another deep breath.

"He also doesn't want strangers in his home every day. So, since both my job and your father's can be done anywhere in the country, it makes the most sense that the three of us move."

Juliana slammed her hand on her lap. "But my life can't just happen somewhere else in the country!"

Her father shot her look, this one telling her to keep it down. "You're a teenager," he replied dryly. "There are thousands of schools in Canada, most with hundreds of students for you to choose your friends from. Same with dance studios. Your 'life' can very well be done anywhere in the country."

Juliana propped her elbow on the table and stared at the TV over the bar. Why did Mom have to bring this all up again?

"Tomorrow we'll reach Sault Ste. Marie, and the day after we're in Kitchener," Mom said. "Just one more day."

"Yay," Juliana mumbled to herself.

VAUGHAN.

That's what the sign said. In the car, Juliana's legs were bouncing from not being able to dance all week, but at least her parents had let her sleep in this morning and spend some time in the hotel's pool. She'd even managed to chat with Rachel on WhatsApp for a half hour last night, but then she had to get to bed.

But the city name seemed familiar.

"Why do I know that name?" she asked.

"Vaughan is the city where I did my master's degree in dance," her mother said from the driver's seat.

"What's that again?"

"A lot of research. I investigated representations of the feminine body in Busby Berkley's musicals, theorizing that the images of unified women helped create a new discourse on the ideal feminine form."

Juliana had no idea what her mother had just said, but she was used to it by now. Any time discussion of her mom's dance education came up, so did the topic of her research. And any time Juliana asked Mom to bring it down to her level, as hard as she tried, Mom couldn't. After three minutes of listening to Mom explain it to her, Juliana would just ask her to stop. Juliana of course knew Busby Berkley, the long-dead Hollywood producer responsible for all those incredible chorus-line shots taken from above. But representation? Discourse? Not Juliana's language. Dance was her language: no matter what happened anywhere in her life, or at any time, she could always turn on music and free her emotions from her body. Whether she was happy, sad, frustrated…it didn't matter. That was part of the reason she felt so caged right now: she couldn't let loose while trapped in the SUV with her parents. Even tapping out a rhythm annoyed them. Dance was not something to be contained and analyzed in the mind—it was meant to be lived in and expressed through the body.

"Listen," Dad said, and Juliana braced herself. Any time he said "listen," she knew she was about to get a lecture of some kind. "I know it's been really tough sitting in a car this entire time, especially with us. And I know your whole life has been uprooted." He paused.

"Okay…?" Juliana answered, not sure where he was going with this: it didn't sound like an oncoming lecture.

"We celebrate Christmas Eve tomorrow with Mom's family, then Christmas Day with the Morgans. Then it's Boxing Day. On the twenty-seventh, I have to check in with my new employer, and the moving truck should arrive then, too, but that evening we'll head over to the mall and get you a new SIM card, okay?"

Juliana's eyes popped out of her head.

"I have to wait another four days?"

"Sorry, sweetie," Mom said. "We thought that would be good news. It's just because of all the timing and the holidays. If we try and get you a SIM card on Boxing Day, we'll be in line for hours."

"So?" Juliana asked. Then an idea came to her and her mood lifted immediately. "Oh, all right. I'll just log in to Opa's network."

Dad looked at her through the rearview mirror, "Your opa doesn't own a computer. We've arranged for the Internet to be installed on the twenty-seventh, too."

"What?"

"Don't worry—we're only talking a few days here. We'll be so busy with Christmas you'll hardly notice." Dad tried to elicit a smile from Juliana through the rearview mirror, but she just stared back at him.

She hadn't asked for this move: away from her friends,

the only city she knew, a dance studio she loved…and at Christmas? Juliana stared at her phone. The last text from Rachel, which had just made it through before they'd left the hotel's Wi-Fi network read, *I miss you. Call me as soon as you can.*

Maybe the hotels had actually been better. They at least had had Wi-Fi.

CHAPTER FOUR

The whole family was waiting outside their home, by the sidewalk, for Meier Josef to come by in his sleigh. He'd offered to drop Tata off at the train station in a neighbouring town.

All the children—Elisabeth, Anna, Luki, and Rosina—had tears in their eyes, and their parents didn't seem to notice.

"One of the things I hope we can afford when I return, after I buy us more land is a shingle roof," Tata said. "Herr Meier couldn't stop talking about his after church yesterday. Not a single leak this year."

Why was a shingle roof so important that her father had to leave the family for a dangerous journey to America? Yes, their straw roof leaked in the spring melt, but they could always repair it. Elisabeth would rather deal with that than not have Tata around.

"You can ask him more about it as you drive to the station," Mammi said. "It'll be nice not to have the roof leak when it rains," Mammi said, and Elisabeth frowned. "Lukas, do you have everything in your luggage now?"

Tata patted his trunk. "I have my tools—though I left some important ones with you so you can work while I'm gone. Clothing, shoes, my coat…"

"And your food?"

Tata opened the heavy bag he had hung across his body. "Your bread, sauerkraut, sausage, plum jam, and cheese."

"Two loaves should help you save money for part of the trip," Mammi said.

Tata nodded. "Saving money is what matters so I'm prepared for whatever happens in America. I have the addresses of Meier Josef's friends in Pennsylvania. He said he's written them all to let them know I may be calling. Hopefully I can stay with one of them until I can find boarding."

Many Semlakers had travelled to America over the years, and many had done very well for themselves, sometimes even staying there and bringing their families afterwards. Although Elisabeth wasn't aware of anyone in her family who had made the long and fearful journey, a cousin of Maria's grandmother had moved there maybe twenty years before. Elisabeth had never heard any bad news, but that didn't mean nothing had happened.

"When are you coming back?" Rosina asked through her sniffles.

"Hopefully in a year," Tata replied. "Fewer people died in America because of the war than here. That means more people need shoes."

"I still don't understand why you can't find work in Arad," Elisabeth said, referring to the central city of their region. "There are more people there than in Semlak."

Anna wiped her eyes and nose with the back of her mittened hand.

"Anna!" Mammi scolded. "Use your handkerchief!"

"I don't have one," Anna replied.

Mammi slapped the back of her hand. "You can wash those when we get inside."

Anna's shoulders drooped.

"I expect you to remember your manners while I'm gone," Tata said. "Once I have a place to live, I'll write you all immediately with my address, and then your mother will tell me all about how you've behaved." His face was stern. "God is still watching you, even when I'm not."

The children nodded.

"And your tickets?" Mammi asked, as though nothing had just happened.

Tata unbuttoned his coat to show travel tickets poking out of the pocket inside and then buttoned it back up again.

Elisabeth shivered. The sun hadn't come up yet, and with only an undershirt and blouse underneath her shawl, the morning fall air had reached her bones. A quick glimpse at her sisters told her they felt the same. Little Rosina was shivering, so Elisabeth bade her to come closer and then lifted part of her skirt to the side and extended it around her baby sister. Rosina pulled it tight around her.

"I'm cold, too!" Anna snuggled into Elisabeth, but Elisabeth had no more free fabric to help her.

"You should have brought out another shawl," Mammi said.

"I didn't have time."

"Anna," Tata said, again in his stern voice, "we do not complain of such things. Jesus endured forty days in the desert. A little time in the cold is nothing compared to that."

"I'm fine," Luki said.

"Because you have a coat!" Anna shot back.

"And you have mittens!"

"Enough!" Tata commanded.

Everyone stood in silence and said not a word for a few moments.

Then something dawned on Elisabeth. "I almost forgot!" she said, unwrapping herself from her sisters and running back inside the house. She unlaced her boots at the door in the kitchen so as not to wet the loam-and-straw floor, darted into the front room, grabbed a folded piece of paper and an extra two blankets, rushed back to the kitchen, slipped into her boots, leaving the laces undone, and appeared back outside in a matter of moments. She handed each of her sisters a blanket, ignoring the frown on her parents' faces. Then she passed the paper to Tata.

"Here," she said. "It's your Christmas card. It's from the last page in my drawing book."

On the card's cover was a drawing of Jesus lying in a manger, with Maria and Josef kneeling on either side. Yellow and brown pencil crayon showed the straw that lay on the ground. Above the manger was a yellow star that shone brightly, and the face of an angel peered in from the corner of the page.

Tata's jaw dropped. "Elisabeth…" He showed the card to everyone. The children gasped, and even Mammi nodded approvingly. "You've never drawn anything this lovely," Tata said. He opened up the card and read aloud what Elisabeth had written: "Dear Tata—I promise to keep reading the Bible, the teachings of Martin Luther, and your encyclopedia while you are away. I will do my best to help Mammi, and I will not complain this spring when I must whiten the walls again. I pray that you arrive safely in Pennsylvania and that many friends will be there to help you. Love, Your Lissika."

"My golden one," he said, "thank you. I will keep this in my coat pocket always."

Luki piped up. "I want to give you a hug!"

Tata smiled as Luki wrapped his short, skinny arms

around Tata's middle. Anna and Rosina joined in. All the children began to cry again, and Elisabeth's anger rose up.

"It's not fair!" she said. "We want you to stay! I don't care if the roof leaks! I don't care how much land we have! Leaving your family is wrong!"

Mammi slapped her cheek. "You do not speak like that to your father!"

"I'll hand you the belt when we're back inside," Elisabeth said defiantly. "You didn't die in the war or disappear. You returned. It's not fair that you're leaving us again!"

"Hold your tongue," Tata said. "This is not how I want to remember you, Elisabeth. You are a kind, obedient, pious child, not an angry one possessed by the devil." Elisabeth hung her head in shame. "We must all make sacrifices to survive. Remember that God made the ultimate sacrifice: think of Him before you speak like that again."

He sacrificed His only son, Elisabeth thought, daring not to speak her mind again. *What father does that?* Then she immediately vowed to ask God for forgiveness before bed tonight because of her thoughts.

The *clip-clop* of horses' hooves approached the house. Elisabeth wrapped her shawl tighter around her, not against the cold but to comfort herself with an embrace she needed. Meier Josef pulled up, tipped his hat, and climbed down from his wagon. He shook Tata's hand and nodded to Mammi, and then shook little Luki's hand and nodded to the girls. He looked down at Elisabeth's untied boots.

She knew at least one thing he'd tell everyone about after he returned.

Meier Josef and Tata hoisted the trunk onto the sleigh, and the former took his seat again on the bench at the front. The younger Schuhmacher children cried as they hugged their father one last time. Elisabeth at first held back—if she embraced him, she feared she would break apart. But when Tata opened his arms to her, she couldn't resist. She rushed in and squeezed him so tightly it was as though her body were trying to anchor him here, to keep him from taking that step onto the sleigh and driving off to a new world, one that was so far away it would be many weeks before they knew he had even arrived.

"My golden one, your Tata can't breathe," he said. Embarrassed, Elisabeth pulled away. He lifted her chin with his finger and looked in her eyes the way he did after she had correctly answered all the questions to one of his quizzes.

"You are the oldest," he said. "Be strong. Jesus can help you."

She swallowed and nodded.

Tata and Mammi looked at each other, their faces serious, but Elisabeth caught a glimpse of love in their eyes, which she had seen only once before: not in the wedding photo that hung in the back room, but in one that had been stuffed in a drawer. They embraced—tightly—then separated. Tata climbed onto Meier Josef's sleigh and took one last look around.

"By the time I return, this will all be Romania." He let out a heavy sigh, Meier Josef shook the reins, and the horses trotted off.

"I want to be the golden one," Luki said, pouting as the sound of the horses' hooves grew distant, taking their father from them. "When do I get to be the golden one? I'm the only boy."

No one answered Luki's question as Mammi pushed everyone back inside.

"Elisabeth and Rosina, you clean the breakfast dishes. Luki, I'll help you feed the animals. Anna, wash those filthy mittens."

Anna and Rosina clung to Elisabeth, and Elisabeth didn't know what to do. Like them, her world had just changed. Unlike them, Tata had asked her to be strong.

I don't know if I can, she thought as she looked in the direction the sleigh had gone.

CHAPTER FIVE

Juliana stood in the driveway of the little bungalow that was about to become her new home. The sun was shining, but the winter air in Kitchener was damp and uncomfortable, the ground and trees bare and ugly. Everything said, *This is not your home.*

Juliana didn't know if she could do this.

Dad rang the doorbell at the side door of the small house, and after a few moments, Opa opened it. He was tall but slouched over, the sun reflecting off his shiny head. He wore a plaid shirt, a tan sweater, brown slacks, and brown leather slippers. *Like a grandfather out of the movies,* Juliana thought.

A huge smile lit up his face.

"Katy!" he said as he saw his daughter. Mom smiled

back. They clamped onto each other in a tight embrace, leaving Juliana to hope she wouldn't be stuck in a hug like that. It wasn't that she didn't like Opa—he always sent her cards for her birthday, Christmas, and Easter, and even put money in them—but she only hugged friends. Hugging anyone else, especially adults, was…awkward.

"How are you holding up, Tata?" Mom asked.

"I am doing fine," he said in his mild German accent. Opa shook Dad's hand and their hug was less intense, which gave Juliana a little hope.

"Oh my goodness," Opa said, his smile growing even bigger. "This isn't Yulika, is it?"

She could never figure out why he called her that. She didn't like it, but she didn't have the heart to tell him.

"It is," Mom said, smiling. She didn't correct him, even though she knew Juliana's feelings about the name. Was Juliana going to have to answer to that all the time now?

But it was best to be polite. She was angry at her parents, not her grandfather.

Opa opened up his arms and Juliana wrapped hers around him loosely. He had the old-man smell, so she tried to turn her nose away.

Thankfully, he let her go quickly.

"I know young people don't like to hug," Opa said, "but you were this big when I saw you the last time." He held his arms as though cradling a baby.

He stepped back from the doorway and Juliana could see inside: it opened onto a landing, with a full staircase leading into the basement and two stairs up to the main floor. Each member of the family had to take off their shoes on the tiny landing before going all the way in, and Juliana shivered. This damp, snowless cold in Kitchener was so uncomfortable compared to the dry cold in Calgary.

"Come in, come in!" Opa said as he gestured to the small, round table in the kitchen. "What do you want to drink?"

"You sit, Tata. I'll look after us," Mom said as she took everyone's outerwear and hung everything up in a closet in a hallway off the kitchen.

But Opa would have none of it. "Your modr would be angry if I did not get drinks."

"Motor?" Juliana asked.

Mom laughed. "M-o-d-r. *Modr*. It's what I called my mother." This was new to Juliana. Mom had always said "my mother" when referring to Juliana's grandmother. But since Mom always said "Tata" to talk about her father, this did make sense. It had just never occurred to Juliana that Mom would have a German word for her mother.

Mom looked to her father. "If you insist, but only today."

The kitchen had two small windows: one that looked out over the driveway, and one that looked out to the street. Just to the right of the front window was a dishwasher in seventies green. To its left were low cupboards and the kitchen sink, a tiny area for preparing food, and then the oven with some cupboards above it, the fridge, and finally a cupboard under the side window.

"Yuliana?" Opa asked. He also never said her full name with a *j*. "Would you like some pop?"

Juliana shook her head. "Just water, please, Opa."

"I have juice and milk, too."

"No, thank you. Just water."

Opa gave Mom a confused look and Mom smiled back at him. "She's really into dance, Tata. Now that we're in town, you'll hopefully be able to see her. She's wonderful." She smiled at Juliana and Juliana let the corners of her mouth turn up.

Opa beamed and then reached for a glass out of a cupboard above the dishwasher. It was hard to hold on to any anger around him. He was truly happy to see her. He *wanted* to see her.

To the right of the dishwasher was the house's front door. Now it made sense to Juliana why they had come in the side door: who'd want slushy boots in the kitchen? Beside the door, as part of the next wall, was an opening to the living room, followed by more cupboards—glass ones up top and solid-wood ones below—then another opening to the living room, and then, extending from the kitchen's back wall, the small hallway where Mom had hung every-one's jackets, and likely where the bedrooms and bathroom were. Beside the hallway entrance was a small wall unit with an old telephone hanging beside it, whose numbers were arranged in a circle, and the fattest TV Juliana had ever seen: it almost seemed to be deeper than it was wide.

Opa placed her glass of water in front of her on the table.

"Thank you, Opa," she said.

"So, Peter," Dad said, "the moving truck will be here on the twenty-seventh, and we're getting Internet installed. It'll be a really busy day, but it shouldn't be too bad."

Opa nodded. "I remember, and I have it written down on my calendar." He walked over to the phone and pointed to a small calendar hanging beside it. "Rebecca and Tony moved my things to the basement room a few weeks ago, so my bedroom is ready for the two of you." Rebecca and Tony were Juliana's oldest cousins. Aunt Anne's children. Mom had said they were already out of high school. "And Yuliana, you'll have your mom and aunt's old room. The third bedroom is still for guests."

"I still feel uncomfortable about taking your room," Dad said.

Opa shook his head. "There's only one room downstairs and three up here. A daughter needs to be near her parents."

No, she doesn't, Juliana thought.

"But the guest bedroom…?" Dad asked.

"Guests don't stay in a basement. We didn't do that in the old country."

Mom smiled. "You didn't have a basement in Semlak, Tata. It was for food storage."

Opa thought for a moment and then laughed. "*Stimmt.*"

No one translated for Juliana, and Dad didn't say anything, but Opa's body language suggested he agreed with Mom.

"So, you see? There's nothing wrong with me."

Juliana was beginning to wonder the same thing. Opa seemed perfectly happy and wasn't forgetting anything. Why did they have to come here? Not only was she thousands of kilometres from her friends, but she was in a tiny house with only two bathrooms—she'd have to share one with her parents now. She knew her bedroom was going to be small, too.

"Where can I practise?" Juliana asked. It was the one question her parents kept saying they wouldn't know until they'd arrived.

Well, now they'd arrived.

"How's the rec room in the basement, Tata?" Mom asked.

Opa wrinkled his nose. "I'm sorry…I haven't had time to clean it."

Didn't have time to clean it? What did he do all day? Watch TV on that really old set?

"We'll have to clean the basement first," Mom said, "and then you can try it out. But it'll be a few days before we get to it."

Juliana didn't want to imagine what the rec room—or the entire basement for that matter—looked like. With any luck, her bedroom would at least be big enough for her to stretch and maybe do a little ballet barre in the middle. At this point, she'd settle for almost anything.

IT WAS TEN AT NIGHT, and Juliana lay in her sleeping bag on the floor of her new room. Apparently, Mom and Aunt Anne thought it best to remove the bunk bed that had been in there.

"It was our bed when I was a kid," Mom had said, "and our parents had bought it at a garage sale. So we had no idea how old that frame was…or the mattresses. Besides, your father and I thought you'd want your own bed in here."

Juliana had no issues with an old bed frame. And what was wrong with ordering a new mattress online? Would've been here by now. If anyone had bothered to ask her, she would've told them so. It's not like the carpet she was lying on was new.

"Pretend you're having a sleepover with Rachel," Juliana said to herself.

Hard to do when your best friend wasn't actually there, though.

"Okay. Next 'have fun' attempt. I get to stretch in here so long as my furniture's not here." She sighed. "But once it does come, I'll be barely able to move in this bedroom."

The room was just big enough for her twin bed, desk, chest, and bookshelf. Once her furniture arrived, she'd have to stretch elsewhere in the house. Her room back home had had ample space for furniture and stretching. That made her morning routine super easy: roll out of bed, stretch, get ready for school.

"Hopefully the basement will have more space," she said to herself.

A rumbling sound from the basement travelled through the floor.

It was Opa snoring.

She pulled her portable speakers out of her suitcase and placed them on the floor. She plugged in her phone, opened her music app, and then grunted in frustration.

"'No connection to the Internet,'" she read aloud. "Of course not." She hadn't thought to download music when she'd been connected on the trip.

She tossed her phone onto her pile of clothes. "Why are we even here? Opa seems just fine, this house is way too small for us, my friends are thousands of kilometres away, and I don't even get to graduate from junior high. Not to mention, this city is the ugliest I've ever seen, and all there is around it is farmland. The nearest big city is Toronto… an hour away!" She missed the Rockies and the permanent blanket of snow that stayed on the ground from mid-fall to mid-spring. Outside, Kitchener was dismal: the temperature had hovered just above freezing all day, which explained why the grey sleep of winter that snow always covered in Calgary had been uncovered here.

She grabbed her phone again and opened a book to

where she'd last left off, using her phone's flashlight to help her read. She'd asked her parents about hot spotting to one of their phones—they'd notice her connection if she didn't ask, anyway—but they told her to get to bed because tomorrow would be a busy day.

She needed a connection to her outside world. Why didn't her parents understand that?

CHAPTER SIX

Elisabeth checked to ensure nothing was on the wood-burning stove. The postman was about to arrive in the town, and that meant the week's news and mail.

"I don't want to go," Rosina insisted. "It's cold outside."

"I want to hear the news, and Mammi's in the workshop, still practising on an old pair of shoes. You can't stay in the house by yourself."

Truth be told, Elisabeth wanted to know if Tata had written. Although she was certain he could not have written from Pennsylvania—he was probably still travelling—maybe he had written from Hungary or Austria or Germany to say his trip was going well.

Or maybe the postman would report of a sunken ship when he shared the week's news…

But she of course wouldn't tell that worry to Rosina.

"Put your boots on. I'll get our things."

Elisabeth gathered her and Rosina's shawls and mittens from the back room. The postman would arrive within the half hour. She did not wish to be late. But when she returned to the kitchen, Rosina sat in a chair at the table, sulking.

"I'm not going."

Elisabeth rolled her eyes. Were children this difficult in Jesus's time?

"You don't speak like that to Mammi. Please, Rosina, let's go. I don't want to miss the postman."

"It's cold outside. I'm staying here."

Elisabeth loosened Rosina's boots, which Tata had made, and which now stood by the door at the side of the kitchen. "We must go. Please. I want to find out if the postman knows anything about Tata." There. That should convince her.

But to Elisabeth's surprise, Rosina seemed unmoved.

"Rosina! Don't you want to hear about your father?"

"It's cold outside. I don't want to go outside." And with that, she stomped into the front room and sat on her bed.

How could Rosina be so uncaring toward their father? He had returned from the war just over a year ago, after being gone for two.

"Wait a moment..." Elisabeth said to herself. That meant Rosina had been three when Tata had left for the war. What child had memories of their father before then?

And Tata had spent most of the past year in his workshop, trying to earn money again, or was out on the *salasch*, where the family farmed their year's worth of food, and he often spent time with the men at someone's house or at a tavern. He certainly spent time with the family at many meals and on Sundays. But Rosina was six years old. Elisabeth was fourteen.

Elisabeth looked up at the crucifix hanging in the kitchen. Yes, Rosina knew who her father was. Yes, she missed him. That's why she'd cried when he left just over two weeks ago. But she didn't miss him enough to brave the cold winter for news.

The war had taken away Rosina's father. Just like Rosina didn't remember why the church bells had been taken away, she didn't have many memories with their father.

Anger at that great war swelled inside Elisabeth. What had the Schuhmachers—or any family in Semlak for that matter—done to deserve this? Why did they have to suffer like this, as a separated family, because strangers decided they needed men to fight for them? Elisabeth didn't know what caused the war, only that the Austrian-Hungarian Empire needed men to win it.

"And we lost anyway, and now the empire no longer exists."

She joined Rosina on her bed, bringing her sister's shawl with her. Time was running out. "I know you don't like going out into the cold. But God says we must honour

our father and mother, and Mammi would not let you stay here alone."

Rosina turned her head the other way.

Elisabeth sighed. "I'll do your sweeping for you after lunch."

Rosina grabbed her shawl and ran into the kitchen to her boots.

ELISABETH AND ROSINA, their shawls pulled tightly around their shoulders, hurried down toward the main street. They lived in the northern half of Semlak, as the Lutheran and Calvinist Germans generally did. Germans who moved to Semlak after the initial settlers set roots in the area just outside the village, in what Semlakers called "the new villages." Romanians and other nationalities lived south of the main street.

"I can't run this fast," Rosina complained.

"And I'm not sweeping if we miss the postman."

They turned the corner onto the main road only to stop in their tracks. Directly ahead of them was Georg Schuhmacher, an older cousin on Tata's side.

Rosina hugged Elisabeth's waist. "Did he hear us?"

Georg hadn't turned around.

"I don't think so."

Georg was a tall, strong man, the eldest of their cousins. He, too, had fought in the war. But whereas

Tata had returned in the summer of last year, Georg had made it just in time for Christmas. Mammi, who was actually only a few years older than him, said he had been mean when he was a child. But since returning, Georg suffered from fits and tremors, which Mammi called God's punishment for all the years he had teased and made fun of others. It made sense to Elisabeth: Pastor Fröhlich taught that God punished people who sinned.

Georg appeared to be walking in the direction of the town hall, where the postman would be. But at his slow pace, Elisabeth feared they'd miss the postman if she and Rosina didn't pass Georg. Did he know what time the postman came? What if he was walking somewhere else?

The snow and gravel crunched under their feet.

If Elisabeth and Rosina ran past him, would he have one of those fits? But what if he saw them at the gathering? He'd surely recognize them and know why they had run. Elisabeth was frightened of him, but she didn't want to be rude. That would embarrass not only her but also Mammi and Tata. He would tell his wife, Eva, that Elisabeth and Rosina had run past him, and Eva was another gossipy woman. She would tell everyone at church.

But Elisabeth needed to get to the postman on time. Plus, she was studying for her confirmation, which would happen before Easter. Receiving her confirmation meant she would become an adult in the church. She had better begin acting like one.

"Let's walk quickly," Elisabeth said, "and I'll say hello for both of us."

Rosina pulled herself closer toward her older sister, but Elisabeth pushed her away. "We'll both trip if you do that."

"He scares me."

"I know. But I'm certain he won't hurt you, and we don't want to hurt his feelings. Remember: Tata would be upset if he heard we treated someone from his family poorly."

She clenched her shawl closed with one hand and held onto Rosina's hand with the other. They picked up their pace.

As they passed Georg, Elisabeth looked up and said, "Good day, Georg."

Georg nodded but otherwise said nothing.

Relieved, Elisabeth and Rosina continued on their way. They arrived early.

"Elisabeth!" a voice called out.

Elisabeth smiled as Maria ran up to her. They held hands and smiled at each other.

Maria bent forward and tapped Rosina on her shoulder. "Hello, Rosina. Nice to see you!"

Rosina smiled back.

"How is your family doing?" She looked concerned. Maria enjoyed church gossip like all the other girls, but she was a good friend: her question about Elisabeth's family was genuine.

"We're doing all right."

"We hope to hear about Tata," Rosina added.

Elisabeth pointed to a woman with two children. "Look, Rosina. There's Frau Bartolf with her grandchildren. Why don't you go and play with them."

That was all it took for Rosina to dart off.

This Bartolf family—there were many—lived on the corner of the Schuhmachers' street. The parents, like Tata, had left for Pennsylvania, but did so last year. The grandparents were raising the children.

"To be honest," Elisabeth said, "it's hard. I had to bribe Rosina to come out with me because I couldn't leave her in the house by herself—Mammi's trying to practise how to make shoes, so she's in the workshop—and with Anna and Luki in school, I'm by myself. We don't know if Tata's travels have been good so far…"

Maria rubbed Elisabeth's back. "I'm sure Jesus is keeping him safe."

"I hope so."

Just then, the postman rode in on his horse. He dismounted, pulled his drum out of a saddle bag, hung it around his neck, and began banging on it to draw attention. The children covered their ears at the noise.

Once a crowd had formed, the postman bellowed out the news of the week, most of it headlines from Arad and Temeswar.

"New bill to become law soon! Arad county will be Romanian again!"

Again? What did that mean? But Elisabeth didn't dare

ask. Murmurs rippled through the crowd. The adults probably knew. She would ask someone later.

Elisabeth jumped when a voice called out a question from behind her. It was Georg.

"Any word on prisoners of war being released from Russia?"

The postman shook his head, his expression sad.

Georg walked away, not even waiting for any letters. But when the postman handed out the mail, he had something for Georg.

No one would take it.

So, Elisabeth swallowed and accepted it. She'd deliver it on their way home. *Thou shalt love thy neighbour as thyself.* It's what Jesus would want, right? Then why did she feel so scared? Why wasn't Jesus giving her the courage needed to deliver something to someone who frightened her?

CHAPTER SEVEN

hy did Mom always want Juliana to do something exactly when Juliana didn't want to do it? Like right now: Mom wanted Juliana to socialize.

"I'd rather eat alone," Juliana said.

Mom crossed her arms. "The last thing you need right now is to stay cooped up in your room. Sophie's only two years younger than you, and she's really nice. Besides, she's already here."

Great. Now Juliana felt obligated to come out of her room: Sophie would feel stupid sitting there with three adults, even though she probably had enough difficulties in her life without dealing with a cousin who also didn't want to hang out right now.

Just have fun, Juliana thought, remembering Miss Kasia's advice. She stood up off the floor.

"And Sophie has Stargardt disease: she's losing the ability to see directly in front of her. She can still see plenty, but she may not see all your facial expressions."

Juliana blinked. "Pardon? When were you going to tell me this?"

"She was only diagnosed six months ago. Aunt Anne wanted to keep it private."

Terrific. Juliana had never interacted with someone blind before: she didn't want to say anything that'd make Sophie uncomfortable. A heads-up would've been nice so she could've found some social media activists to learn from first.

If she'd had the Internet.

Juliana followed Mom into the kitchen.

Sophie sat at the small kitchen table while Aunt Anne finished serving some deli sandwiches and chips. Opa sat there, too, simply beaming.

"It's so nice to have more of my family here." His gaze moved between his daughters and granddaughters. Juliana had to admit, his happiness was infectious. A smile crept onto her face.

"Yulika," Opa said, "this is Sophie. She's your cousin."

"Hi," Juliana said.

"Hi," Sophie replied, staring at her hands.

"Why don't you sit next to each other?"

Juliana caught an exchange of concerned looks

between Mom and Aunt Anne. What was wrong? But Juliana followed Opa's lead and sat beside Sophie.

"Sophie likes skiing and wall climbing," Aunt Anne said.

"Oh." Juliana laughed nervously. "I'd be scared of falling and breaking something."

Sophie's lips tightened, and Juliana caught another fleeting look of concern from her aunt. Had Juliana already said something wrong?

"What Juliana probably meant," Aunt Anne said, "was that she'd be worried about breaking something and not being able to dance."

Sophie's cheeks turned red, though if from anger or embarrassment, Juliana couldn't tell, so she bit into her sandwich to kill the awkward silence that had engulfed the tiny kitchen.

"Good sandwich."

Why did parents always make things worse? She and Sophie would've figured things out on their own. Yes, Juliana was nervous because of Sophie's eye condition—a lot of disability activists online were tired of people treating them like helpless humans, so Juliana didn't want to say something wrong, which she obviously had. But she was also certain the two of them would've found something to talk about eventually.

"Mom's a good cook," Sophie replied.

"My mom tries."

Mom looked insulted. "Hey!"

Opa laughed. "And you work in a grocery store."

"Yes, and not a restaurant. Be careful, Tata. I'm cooking for you now, not Annie. I can cook worse if you're not nice."

Phew. Situation saved.

"Since Juliana's new here, Sophie," Mom said, "your mom and I thought it might be fun if you showed her around the neighbourhood."

We thought you might want to be her friend. Ugh. Did they not get it? *Stop trying to force things!*

Opa smiled and nodded. "That sounds like a wonderful idea! Family should help each other."

Just because we're family doesn't mean we're going to like each other, Juliana thought. Was Sophie thinking the same thing?

Sophie took another bite of her sandwich. Was it just because? Or to avoid answering? Either way, avoiding an answer was a good idea, so Juliana bit into hers, too.

Of course, spending time with Sophie could be a chance to get to know each other on their own terms, away from the adults. Juliana didn't know anyone, and since Sophie was the only cousin from that family of six here, that suggested she was the only girl closest to Juliana in age. It would be nice to have someone who was kind of like a sister.

Assuming they got along, of course.

"You know what?" Aunt Anne said. "Why don't they go to Mr. Casimiro's for dessert?"

Mom's eyes popped out of her head. "Oh, that sounds like a fabulous idea! I haven't been in years!"

Juliana stared at both of them, but now even Sophie smiled. "But can we go by ourselves? Juliana's fourteen."

Taking advantage of Juliana's age to get rid of the parents. Juliana liked how Sophie thought.

Mom and Aunt Anne hesitated, but Opa answered immediately. "Yes, Sophie, you are going by yourselves. Young people like you and Yulika don't need old people like us following you all the time."

Opa was the first adult in Juliana's family to act like her cheerleader. He stood up. "I am giving you some money. Finish your sandwiches. Then you can go." He pointed a finger at his daughters. "And do not argue with your father."

Huh. Juliana could get used to Opa. She ate as quickly as she could change costumes at a dance competition.

AFTER LUNCH, Aunt Anne and Mom did indeed listen to their father and allow Juliana and Sophie to go out alone, which surprised Juliana. That would've never happened in Calgary: her mom was too nervous to let her go anywhere alone except to and from school and to Rachel's place. However, this diner was indeed just two minutes away. That must've helped convince Mom to let Juliana go without any adults. It was across the street, up a path, through a parking lot, and across another street. A minute later, they sat inside a really cute diner that looked like it came out of the musical *Grease*: it had a pink, black, white, and chrome colour scheme but with tables and chairs that looked modern with their clean and simple lines. Orderly, just how Juliana liked it.

This was perhaps the first really good thing that had happened to Juliana since leaving Calgary.

An older gentleman with thinning hair smiled as he approached.

"Miss Sophie! Nice to see you! Merry Christmas!"

Sophie smiled. "Merry Christmas, Mr. Casimiro. This is my cousin, Juliana."

"Your cousin? But your uncle doesn't have…"

Mr. Casimiro thought for a moment and then his eyes lit up. "Is Katy here?"

He knew Juliana's mom? So that's why Mom seemed excited to come and why she allowed Juliana to come here. She knew the owner.

Sophie nodded.

Mr. Casimiro grabbed Juliana's hand and shook it vigorously. "Please tell your mother to come by and say hello as soon as she can. I haven't seen her in such a long time! Do you know she loved my wife's *polvo à la lagareiro* when she was young?"

Sophie furrowed her brow, and Juliana shook her head in uncertainty.

"It's a famous Portuguese dish made from octopus," Mr. Casimiro said.

Octopus? Mom eats octopus? What kind of diner offers octopus? Where has my family sent me?

"Unfortunately, tastes have changed over the decades. We don't offer it anymore." Mr. Casimiro handed them both a menu. "We've just updated our menu." Although Juliana was relieved to see the usual fair—burgers, for example—the desserts sounded like a blast. How could she say no to Belmont Blizzard Chocolate Cake? The description said it had peppermint and bits of cranberry. That would hit the spot after everything she'd been through. Besides, it was Christmas. Her health was important to her—eating well supported her dance. But she knew it was important to treat herself, too.

She ordered it.

"And Miss Sophie?"

Sophie perused the menu and then closed it. "I'll have what Juliana's having."

Mr. Casimiro took their menus away and left to get their orders.

"Listen," Juliana said, "thanks for taking me out of that house. After spending almost a week inside a car with my parents, that house isn't much bigger. I was suffocating. I didn't want to see anyone, but I didn't want to stay there."

Sophie laughed. "I've got five siblings. I totally get it. You want to be alone, but with people who aren't your family."

Juliana laughed along. "Because, you know, that makes sense."

"Of course it does!"

Then they fell silent, realizing they had nothing in common if Juliana danced and Sophie enjoyed other sports.

Sophie finally spoke. "So, um, what's it like in Calgary?"

"Well…the Rockies aren't too far away. You'd probably enjoy climbing them…? Oh! And the snow falls and stays. It's not like this…whatever you call this season here. And never confuse a Calgarian with an Edmontonian. Then there's this horrible feeling that I'm betraying my province by living this close to Toronto."

"Toronno."

"That's what I said."

Sophie shook her head. "You pronounced the second *t*. Now that you live here, you're no longer allowed to pronounce it. *Toronno*."

Now Juliana laughed. "Are you telling me I have an accent?"

"Yup!"

Was Sophie only this relaxed away from her mom? Or had things been that awkward because of the forced introduction and she was normally this easygoing? *I guess only time will tell*, Juliana thought.

Mr. Casimiro brought their cakes, and the girls dug in and talked about the differences between their provinces, which eventually turned into the differences between their moms. They ended up having a lot to talk about.

After they left, Sophie headed straight home, and Juliana returned to her house, feeling lighter than she had in days.

"You look happier," Mom said.

"You ate octopus?"

Mom chuckled. "I did. When the Portuguese make it, it's delicious."

Juliana passed on Mr. Casimiro's greetings, and Mom said she'd be sure to drop by after Christmas.

"But there's one thing I don't get," Juliana said. "When he handed us the menu, she read it. How can she if she's losing her sight?"

Mom immediately looked worried. "I hope you didn't say anything."

"No, why?"

"What did she order?"

"Same as me."

Mom paused, like she was measuring her words before she spoke.

"Mom, I can tell you're debating something. What is it?"

Mom looked at her daughter for another moment before speaking. "Sophie can't read regular print anymore, but Annie says she pretends to so she can look normal."

That made sense to Juliana in more ways than one. Kids could be cruel—she'd seen her share of bullying in junior high. And most kids tried in some way to fit in. Juliana's biggest fear right now was her first days at dance and school. She knew those paled in comparison to losing your eyesight, but the fear of becoming an outcast—no matter the reason—was very real to all kids her age.

"I get that. So why couldn't you just tell me that? Why the secret?"

"It didn't seem appropriate to share that with you. It's very private."

"Given that Sophie acted like that right in front of me, it's hardly private. How am I supposed to be friends with her if I don't know something that important? I could've kept embarrassing her—"

Mom crossed her arms and set her jaw. "Sophie's situation is extremely sensitive, Juliana, and you wear your emotions on your sleeve. I wasn't sure you'd say something later on."

Juliana's anger swelled in her chest. "You mean, I wear my compassion on my sleeve? My understanding? That's what Rachel and all my friends back at home keep telling me."

"Annie's been having difficulties with Soph—"

"Maybe because Sophie's tired of being talked down to."

Mom took a deep breath. "She's only twelve and going through a tough transition."

Only twelve. Juliana had certainly heard *only* before

her age often enough. When did adults stop using *only* with their children like that?

"Mom, if I had Internet, within ten minutes I could read first-hand experiences from other people losing their eyesight on social media."

Mom's eyes opened wide. "You are *not* talking about your cousin on social media."

Juliana threw her hands in the air. "How stupid do you think I am? Of course I'm not going to invade her privacy like that! Declan at dance has ADHD and autism. Several in my group belong to the queer community. Lots of kids in my grade are disabled. They all talk about how they found their communities online: people their age, mentors, activists, all of it. And their discussions are available for anyone to read. *I can learn from others without asking Sophie a ton of annoying questions.* That's my point. But if you want to make assumptions about me because I'm *only* fourteen, go for it."

Juliana stormed off to her room.

On the one hand, adults created embarrassing situations, like forcing kids to sit next to each other under the assumption they'd get along because they were in the same family. But then they didn't share something important like how someone couldn't read a menu because of a disability, possibly creating more embarrassing situations.

Of course Juliana wouldn't have made a scene. But she could've asked Mr. Casimiro what he recommended. Or she could've asked Sophie what she liked, or her opinion about one or two menu items. Those options would've worked because Juliana was the new girl in town. Reading the entire menu out loud would've been obvious, but there were ways to give Sophie some choice while they were getting to know each other.

Juliana would tell Sophie at some point that she knew about her eyesight—she hated keeping secrets from people—but it wasn't something you talked about the first time you got away from adults. At least, not unless the disabled person raised the subject, and Sophie hadn't raised the subject. Declan had talked about that, too.

If there was one thing her generation had that her parents hadn't at her age, it was immediate access to knowledge on the Internet. Yes, it had its dark corners, but Juliana used it to help her learn about others.

It was basic decency as far as she was concerned.

CHAPTER EIGHT

*E*lisabeth wiped her hands on her apron, an old one that tied around her waist—like all aprons did—and had fraying embroidery along the bottom. It had once been her great-grandmother's Sunday apron, but over the years it had become worn. With a little trimming and repairing, Mammi had turned it into a decent work apron for Elisabeth.

"Anna," Elisabeth said, chopping carrots at the kitchen table, "get me two jars of sauerkraut." Anna nodded, slipped on her boots, and ran around the house to the cellar. "And Rosina, sweep under the table again—I can still see some crumbs."

Rosina dutifully wet a cloth and dampened the floor underneath the table to avoid kicking up dust. She then picked up the broom, which Mammi had shown Elisabeth how to make from the tassels of broom corn after last harvest, from the corner of the kitchen and began sweeping, the long handle threatening to bump her in the nose from time to time as she tried to manoeuvre it like an adult.

"Don't forget the corners, by the legs," Elisabeth said. "Jesus will be born tonight and Mammi's family is coming tomorrow." And Rosina swept harder.

Mammi was in the yard tending to the poultry and had instructed Elisabeth to take care of the kitchen. There was still so much to do before Christmas Eve celebrations could begin: prepare vegetables for a dumpling soup, wash potatoes for peeling and cutting, prepare the dressing for the goose for tomorrow, keep the oven hot...the list of tasks never ended, and they had just washed up the morning's breakfast dishes. Tata had been gone for nearly four weeks now, and although men didn't help with household chores or most Christmas preparations, with him gone, it still seemed like there was more work to be done.

"Cornstalks!"

Luki, who was playing in the front room, and Rosina, stopped to look at her.

"I have to get cornstalks," she explained, and promised herself she'd get them after she was done with the carrots. She still had time.

The oven! She needed to wipe down the oven before Mammi returned. Made of brick and covered in a white lime mixture, dirt showed on it easily.

"Luki, take that cloth in the bucket and wipe down the oven. I want to make sure it's perfectly white."

A mischievous smile crossed Luki's lips. "You have to do that."

Elisabeth sighed. Why did he have to be like this today of all days? Couldn't he wait until after Christmas to be a boy again?

Anna returned, placed the two jars of sauerkraut on the kitchen table, and immediately set to work, helping Elisabeth chop.

"Luki," Elisabeth said, "the *stornickels* will give you coal tonight instead of a gift. Go wipe down the oven."

"No, they won't. Boys don't clean in the kitchen, so I'm not doing anything wrong. I'll be able to say my prayers when they come to our house, so I'll get my gift."

Luki sat defiantly on the ground.

"You're going to make your pants dirty!"

If Tata were here, he'd be teaching him a popular card game or otherwise keeping him occupied, maybe even collecting the cornstalks himself, just to help. But Elisabeth didn't want to send Luki into the stalls alone—he'd definitely come out filthy.

"You have to wash them anyway, so it doesn't matter," Luki said, standing up with a devilish grin on his face, and Elisabeth wanted nothing more now than to pull out that box of dried corn kernels herself and watch him kneel in it for five minutes.

"Elisabeth!"

Elisabeth jumped. She had been so busy with Luki that she hadn't even heard Mammi come in. When she turned around, she could feel herself shrinking on the inside: Mammi was carrying a bushel of cornstalks in her arms. Elisabeth was one more transgression away from the belt.

Forgive me, Jesus: I'm just trying to prepare our meal for You quickly. I was going to get the stalks. You know I was, right?

Elisabeth wiped her hands on her apron and rushed over to take the bushel out of her mother's hands. "Mammi, Luki won't wipe down the oven like I've asked him to."

Mammi slipped out of her boots and into her house shoes and folded her shawl as she took it to the back room to put away.

"You've asked your brother to do your chore? Really, Elisabeth. Your brother will never need to wipe down the oven, so there's no point in making him do it now."

Luki's grin couldn't have been more triumphant, nor Elisabeth's scowl any angrier. Wasn't a good Christian simply supposed to help? Why did it matter if a boy or a girl wiped the oven? She opened the oven door, shoved the glowing coals to the side with the poker, and then stuffed the bare cornstalks in.

"Do I have to sweep that, too?" Rosina asked, looking at the tiny scraps and peels from the stalks that had fallen onto the floor.

"Of course you do," Mammi answered as she headed to

the kitchen table to chop vegetables. "A woman's work is never done."

"But I didn't make that mess!"

Mammi banged the handle of her knife on the table, and everyone jumped. "We are a family. That means we help each other, no matter who did what. We're celebrating Christmas Eve tonight, that means the birth of Jesus, our saviour. Do not complain about something as meaningless as sweeping."

Sulking, Rosina dragged her feet over to the oven door and swept up all the tiny pieces—while kicking up some dust from the floor with the broom—and threw them into the oven, too. She then joined Mammi and Anna at the kitchen table.

If we help each other, Elisabeth thought, *why couldn't Luki wipe the oven?* But she knew better than to ask her question aloud.

She stopped for a moment to see what still needed to be done: the other three certainly didn't need her help, and she had no desire to wipe down the oven right now. All sixteen underskirts were starched and pressed, as well as Luki's vest and pants—she had taken care of that over the past few days. She couldn't start on the goose until the vegetables were done. Baking had been done over the past month and was in the cellar at the back of the house.

"I'll polish everyone's shoes," she said. She laid out a rag rug in the front room, by her bed, found everyone's dress shoes, placed them on the rug, took her father's black polish and a cloth from a drawer in the dresser, then stopped.

Mammi's shoes were the biggest now. Elisabeth had momentarily forgotten about her father's absence, but now the memory returned, ramming into her with the force of a farmer's wagon piled high with harvested wheat. Elisabeth began to cry. She retrieved a handkerchief from her drawer, and Tata's encyclopedia set caught her eye. Elisabeth pulled down one volume and looked up America. She sat on her bed and stared at the map. Even though she had practically memorized it, every time she saw it, she wished it was somehow closer to Hungary, or Romania, or whatever country she lived in now. But the map hadn't changed and Tata was still gone.

"Elisabeth?" Mammi's footsteps pounded into the room. Mammi grabbed the book out of her hands, slammed it shut, and returned it to the shelf. Elisabeth expected the belt.

"You don't have time for this anymore," Mammi said through gritted teeth.

Elisabeth dropped her chin and wiped her eyes and nose with her handkerchief. "I know. I'm sorry. These next few days will be very busy."

"That's not what I mean," Mammi said. Elisabeth looked up. "You don't have time for these books. With your father gone, I must run his business after Christmas. And since you will be confirmed next year, it's time you were in charge of the household: cleaning, cooking, looking after Rosina. And you'll also be helping Luki and Anna with their schoolwork."

"But…" Elisabeth already helped a lot with the household, like any other girl her age. She didn't want to believe what she was hearing and quickly sought another answer. She needed to read her books: they taught her so much about the world. "I can read after they've gone to sleep."

Mammi shook her head. "Not any longer. After the younger ones are in bed, you'll be busy sewing with me. You may have stopped growing, but your siblings haven't."

Elisabeth's jaw dropped.

"You're almost a woman," Mammi said. "After your confirmation, you will start to find a husband, though it may still be hard because of the war: too many men have died and not all have returned from the camps." A look of sadness flew across her face, but it disappeared as quickly as it had appeared. "You're still not fast enough or good enough in your duties."

"I am very good…" Elisabeth began to defend herself.

"If you're polishing shoes, then where are the boots?"

With that, Mammi returned to the kitchen.

Elisabeth stamped out of the front room and into the kitchen and scooped up everyone's boots.

"Be nice," Luki said. "Jesus is coming."

Elisabeth threw her brother a look that frightened even him and returned to the front room. She wiped her cloth in the small canister of polish and began rubbing Mammi's shoes, her hand going faster and faster, until her muscles became too sore. Then she switched hands. And so she continued, rubbing until one arm hurt and then the other, until the pain in her arms matched the anger in her heart.

Even at Christmas.

CHAPTER NINE

Uncle Peter and Brian. Aunt Anne and Uncle Phillip. Rebecca. Tony. Charlie. Dean. Sophie. Scott. Opa. Mom and Dad.

In this small house.

Christmas music blaring out of some old radio.

And Juliana.

In her bedroom.

The door closed.

Unsuccessfully trying to drown out the noise with her earbuds as she watched a video from her dance studio's goodbye party.

She'd had a lot of fun with Sophie yesterday, but Sophie was one person. When Juliana had heard the entire Morgan family pack itself into Opa's tiny kitchen, her insides filled with panic and she parked herself on her sleeping bag in her puny, thin-walled bedroom.

Juliana hated being the new kid on the block, let alone the new kid in the family. She didn't want all the attention. It meant pressure to put on a performance for the next three or four hours… It was Christmas. She just wanted to be herself.

And "herself" was sad, angry, and needing to dance it all out. No one had asked her thoughts about any of this. She was expected to be the good girl and just go along for the ride. It had been so fun spending time with Sophie yesterday, just hanging out, no adults to debate or be hurt by or to remind her yet again why they'd moved thousands of kilometres away from home.

She hit pause on the video, got off her bed, and walked around her room, feeling too antsy to sit still any longer. Without her own practice studio in the house, she had nowhere to release all her pent-up energy. She jumped up and down, trying to shake things out, but the floor creaked. Juliana worried she'd break a hole in it as the mirror hanging on the closet door jiggled in its ancient, plastic brackets. She couldn't dance in here without worrying about bringing the house down.

Looking at herself in the mirror, Juliana smoothed the A-line skirt of her favourite red dress, which was fitted in the bodice and had broad straps that curved over her shoulders. Mom always said she looked lovely in that dress and that it highlighted her brown hair.

The noise from outside quieted down for a moment, and Juliana wondered what was going on. Maybe she should join them. It was Christmas, after all, and she was here, and there was nothing that could be done about it. But she didn't want a crowd. Just alone time with her parents like it had always been at home. Couldn't she have *one* thing the same? Just one?

A knock interrupted her thoughts. Mom entered, and she looked concerned as she closed the door behind her and leaned against the wall. Juliana kept her distance. She wanted to spend time with her parents, not be glued to them.

"It's a lot, isn't it?" Mom said.

Juliana nodded. She could feel tears starting to well up and she tried to push them back.

"You know, this is how I celebrated Christmas, with my family on Christmas Eve."

Juliana nodded to signal she'd heard.

"And how your opa celebrated. My ancestors, too."

Since when did Mom care about her heritage? "You've never talked about that. Why does it matter now?"

"I never talked about it because it rarely did matter to me. We named you Juliana to break with tradition."

Juliana had never heard that before. Evidently, her confusion registered on her face, and Mom continued.

"Every child in your opa's family is named after a family member or a close friend. In your case, you should've probably been named Katherina, Rosina, or Anne. Or Irmgard, after your grandmother."

Juliana smiled at her grandmother's name. She couldn't picture herself as an Irmgard.

"I love my name," Mom continued, "and I love you, but I wouldn't have wanted two of us in the house with the same name."

"And Paul if I was a boy?"

"Paul Junior, most likely. Or Peter, after Opa, or Lukas, after his uncle or grandfather." Mom smiled, too. "My god. Could you imagine calling you Peter? There'd be three of you. But your middle name comes from Tata's mother. We just anglicized the spelling: Elizabeth. She spelled it with an *s*."

A huge explosion of laughter sounded from the kitchen and the family room, and both Mom and Juliana looked in its direction.

"Your Uncle Peter must've just told another one of his travel stories." She paused. "But we're here now for Tata. So we need to do more things that are important to him so long as he can remember them, and he wants to remember more of you. When are you coming to join us?"

Juliana shrugged. "Whenever." Should she tell her mom she'd rather wait until they were all gone? Juliana had just arrived a couple of days ago. It's not like she'd known them her whole life. She felt for Opa, but she mattered, too.

Didn't she?

"I know you're going through a lot," Mom said. "But everyone's asking where my daughter is, and it's…" She hesitated and Juliana felt Mom's lighter mood evaporate. "It's quite frankly embarrassing that you're in here."

Seriously? That was why Mom had come in here? To tell Juliana that she was being rude when it was Mom who was expecting Juliana to do an about-face and pretend like everything was fine?

She sat back down on her sleeping bag and shoved her earbuds back into her ears. "You and Dad had all the time before you told me about the move to get used to the idea." Her voice got louder. "I had three months, and you didn't even ask me what I thought about it!"

Mom straightened up. "Because to pretend to give you a choice would've been a lie. My father needs care, Juliana. We had to move here."

"Is that what you told Dad? 'Paul, we have to move'?" Mom's expression told Juliana everything she needed to know. "That's what I thought. You *asked* him, didn't you? And because I'm just a kid, you didn't ask me. And now you want me to put on a happy face and perform the 'good little daughter' out there for everyone? Dream on."

Mom's jaw dropped and her eyes opened wide. "How dare you speak to your mother like that!"

"And how dare you drag your daughter across the country like that and force me to live with people I don't know!"

"Of course you know your Opa Schuhmacher!"

"Hardly! He sent me nice cards and money in the mail and said a few words to me over the phone!"

Mom straightened herself up and drilled her gaze into Juliana's. "As your dad and I have said, you're not the only one going through a transition here. Now, there's an entire family out there happy to get to know you. Dean is exactly your age, Charlie's just…" Mom counted for a moment. "Charlie's just three years older. I get that Scott might be too young for you—he's only eight—and Tony's in university, and Rebecca too—but you could at least make an effort. Besides, Sophie's wondering where you are."

Mom let out an angry sigh and Juliana returned her attention to her phone. She'd apologize to Sophie later, because she was certain Sophie would understand.

"And whenever you do talk to Sophie, leave your phone alone. She can't tell you're looking at it."

Mom left in a huff, leaving the door open behind her. All the boisterous sounds from the kitchen flooded into Juliana's room.

Furious, Juliana slammed the door shut—the noise from the kitchen was so loud she was certain no one had heard—and returned to her sleeping bag.

She continued watching the video. Even just a quick phone call with Rachel would make her feel so much better. But she didn't know how to use Opa's phone. Besides, everyone would see her talking to Rachel.

"I could hot spot to Mom or Dad's phone and use WhatsApp…" But they probably had all sorts of notifications set and would find out. Plus, it was Christmas Eve. Rachel usually needed it for last-minute present prep herself.

Juliana's door opened, startling her again.

"Juliana?" It was Sophie.

"Oh, hey," Juliana replied.

"Sorry to bug you, but based on how your mom said 'teenagers' to my mom just now, I thought maybe I'd come and see if you're okay."

Juliana rolled her eyes. When Sophie didn't react, she realized her cousin probably hadn't noticed the small reaction. "Parents. Sheesh."

"Yeah. My family never stops paying attention to me, so I kind of get that they're a lot. But I can leave if you want."

"No, that's okay," Juliana said, and glanced at her phone. The frame she'd paused at held her frozen in the worst imaginable position: just after takeoff into a grand jeté, when she looked more like a bug flying through the air than a graceful human.

"Um, I don't have anything to sit on except my sleeping bag. But you can join me."

Sophie smiled. "Kind of like a sleepover, only with my weird family staying, too."

Juliana couldn't help but smile, then caught Sophie's silent reaction again. "That's actually pretty funny. Though I don't know your family. Well, except your mom." She felt bad for her comment. "Sorry. I didn't mean to insult your family. I'm sure they're really nice."

"Oh, no, they're weird. Are you watching something on your phone?" Sophie reached for it.

"A video of me dancing at my going-away party in Calgary."

"Can I watch it?"

"Sure." Should she bring up what she knew about Sophie not being able to read normal print? Juliana decided against it. She hated when her parents broached subjects she wasn't ready to talk about. Besides, this wasn't regular print; it was a video. And Juliana's phone was a larger model. Maybe that changed things.

She reset the video. But as Sophie watched it, Juliana noticed that Sophie did react at appropriate times, like a small gasp when Declan kicked his face, or a smile when Juliana did that full grand jeté. But she was looking a little off to the side, probably using her peripheral vision to watch the video.

Glad I didn't bring up that topic. That would've embarrassed Sophie.

After the number was over, Sophie handed Juliana's phone back. "That was amazing! Are you going to dance here again?"

Juliana nodded and then answered. "Yeah. At Kitchener Dance Academy. I can't wait."

"Juliana," Mom called from the hallway, "I need your help in the kitchen. Now."

"The kitchen? Ugh."

Sophie tipped her head to one side. "What's wrong with that?"

"That's my most despised room in the house. You spend all this time preparing food only to mash it into your mouth and never see it again."

Sophie laughed.

Juliana raised her arms. "What? Why go through all that trouble when you can just bite into an apple, shove meat into the oven and let it cook, and then eat it, or shovel a handful of nuts into your mouth? I mean, why rip lettuce leaves into a salad? Just rip off the leaf from the head and bite it!"

Sophie doubled over in stitches.

CHAPTER TEN

*E*lisabeth rushed out of the cellar, across the back of the house, and then along the side, under the overhang. She stamped the snow off her shoes before entering, passed the sausages she'd retrieved to Anna, and then returned to the cellar.

Christmas Eve service would be at seven o'clock, which meant supper and gifts at about five and getting herself and her sisters ready starting sometime after three. It was already after one, and her never-ending list…was still not ending.

Elisabeth's heart was racing in panic. Moreover, they had to prepare for Christmas Day, which included hosting Mammi's family and visiting Tata's. Each of the Braun siblings (Mammi's maiden name was Braun) took turns, and with seven of them before the war, the full Braun family hadn't visited the Schuhmachers for Christmas since 1912. Elisabeth tried to count in her head how many would be coming.

Resi-Néni has had four children since then, but two died. Gretchen-Néni had twins, but one died, like Anna's had... She continued counting, adding and subtracting as she rhymed off her mother's siblings, remembering though, too, that Adam-Bátschi and Andreas-Bátschi had died in the war, so their families would be celebrating with their other side of the family on Christmas Day. Although Elisabeth still missed her aunts and cousins at family Christmas, it had been two years since Andreas-Bátschi's death and four since Adam-Bátschi's. The new traditions had already taken hold.

But another tradition needed to be created: who would sit at the head of the table and carve the goose in Tata's absence?

She retrieved several small rounds of homemade cheese and darted back around the house and into the kitchen.

Twenty-five people, she'd finally calculated.

Elisabeth held out the cheeses to her mother.

"I wanted the freshly smoked meat from the attic," Mammi said, her voice firm and angry. "You were to get the cheese later. I don't have space in the kitchen for it yet." Elisabeth ran back around to the cellar and lay the rounds back on their shelves. She then lifted her skirts with one hand and began ascending the rickety stairs into the attic.

"This would've been Tata's responsibility," she said. "Luki should be doing this." Even though Luki was now the "man" of the house, at only eight years old, he was spared from carrying things up and down those old stairs.

And he's certainly too young to sit at the head of the table, she thought.

The smoke from the oven in the kitchen below floated up the chimney, some of it escaping through the opening in the flue where Mammi had hung sausage to smoke that Tata had made from the last *schlachtfest*, when everyone worked together to butcher pigs and prepare most of their pork for the year to come. The loam-and-straw floor always scared Elisabeth: even though it was thick and supported by rafters, she still feared it would one day soften and she'd fall through.

She tiptoed through the smoke to the hooks where meat was hung to air out a little before being carried down to the cellar. She pulled several links down, hung them around her neck, and headed back down the ladder. She then grabbed a basket of potatoes from the cellar—she knew Mammi would appreciate having those in the kitchen already, and the basket could sit out of the way, under the table—and hobbled to the front door, laden as she was with all the food.

"Rosina," Elisabeth called to her sister, and her youngest sibling ran over and carried some of the smoked sausages.

"Is that all for now, Mammi?" Elisabeth asked.

Mammi nodded, and Elisabeth switched out her boots for her house shoes and quickly washed her hands in the water bowl by the door.

"Now, get the back room ready," Luki commanded, and Elisabeth scowled at him.

"What are you waiting for?" Mammi said. "He's right."

Elisabeth grabbed a clean cloth from the basket in the kitchen and began polishing—for the third time in a week —all the furniture.

"And remember to place all your Sunday clothing in the front room!" Mammi shouted through the kitchen door.

As much as Elisabeth wanted to clean the house so that God and Jesus would be proud of her, her patience was wearing thin. "That's the fifth time she's told me today," she grumbled to herself. Elisabeth would have carried the family's best clothing to the front room earlier, but flour had covered much of the kitchen from Mammi's bread baking that morning, and Mammi insisted Elisabeth wait until the kitchen had been cleaned. But by then, Elisabeth had become busy with her many other chores.

"Did you hear me?" Mammi was getting angrier by the moment.

"Yes!" Elisabeth replied, louder than was needed.

Within moments, Mammi appeared in the doorway.

"Do not shout at me like that! Remember the commandment: honour thy father and thy mother!"

Elisabeth shot a look of defiance at her mother. "It

would be easier if Tata were here instead of in America just to earn money!"

Mammi's mouth and eyes opened wide. "At least you know where your father is! Have you forgotten your uncles? And what about the Kaisers? They still haven't found Kaiser Hans or young Markus yet! You should be grateful Tata returned from the war!"

"And what if he doesn't return from America?" Elisabeth surprised even herself with her question.

Mammi's face turned red, and Elisabeth knew a storm was coming her way. Her siblings, just past Mammi in the kitchen, also had their eyes glued to the argument.

But nothing happened. Or rather, Mammi did nothing. Her face suddenly became pale again and her lips thinned into the tight line she normally held them in.

"He will be back." Her voice was almost a whisper. "Because I will not have another man raising my children."

With that, Mammi turned on her heel and marched into the kitchen.

"Back to work," she barked at everyone.

ELISABETH HAD FINISHED POLISHING ALL the furniture in the back room and was now carrying everyone's Sunday clothes through the kitchen and to the front room.

She felt guilty about what she'd said to Mammi. Elisabeth already knew the answer to the question, and she knew that asking it would hurt Mammi. Why had she asked it?

Returning to the back room, Elisabeth looked up at the crucifix over the doorway.

Did You ever yell at Your father or mother like that?

Elisabeth knew the answer to that, too: no. But with everything Jesus wanted to do, how did He make His wishes clear to His parents?

She pulled Anna's underskirts and outer skirt out of the wardrobe.

Elisabeth knew that no wife wanted to think about the death of her husband any more than a child wanted to think about the death of her father. For a wife, it meant having to marry again quickly. For children, it meant having to learn how to be around a man who wasn't their father but who now stood in that role. After the war, there had been a rash of weddings for many of the widows, and from what Anna and Luki sometimes heard at school, those marriages didn't always work well for the children.

But at least they have someone, Elisabeth thought. Often, wives—like Frau Kaiser—who didn't know if their husbands were alive or dead, were forced to wait for some kind of confirmation before marrying again. Even though brothers and older sons helped, these families still toiled harder than the others who knew what had happened to the head of their family.

The Schuhmachers were by no means a rich family, but they also weren't destitute. They had a house, some farmland, enough money for food they couldn't grow, and Tata's shoemaking business meant he could earn money through the winter, too. Yes, their roof was made of chaff and wire, but Hungarian Germans had lived like that for over a century, many for at least two. Her father's life was worth more to her than a roof or more land.

Did Georg ask if anyone had returned from…what words did he use? Prisoner-of-war camps? Mammi had talked about the camps, too. Did Georg ask because he was waiting for someone? But his father was here, so was his brother Samuel, although he hadn't fought in the war because he was lame… It didn't make sense to Elisabeth.

At the very least, Elisabeth could take comfort when she fell asleep at night for the past year, knowing her father was alive, and his presence had greeted her every morning. She no longer had that certainty. She assumed he was safe, though. The families of those who had gone missing in the war were hoping their loved ones were alive, but they probably assumed they were dead.

That was much worse.

Elisabeth felt Jesus's eyes looking down on her again. *But no matter what I was feeling, I was still wrong to yell at Mammi like that.*

Anna's skirts in her arms, Elisabeth stopped in the kitchen, where Mammi was cleaning up the last of the cooking dishes.

"Keep moving," Mammi said. "There's no time for idling."

But Elisabeth stayed put, her arms overbrimming with the white skirts. "I'm sorry," she said. "I don't want you to be angry with me, and I don't want Jesus to be angry with me, either. I just miss Tata."

Mammi nodded, acknowledging she'd heard, and then waved Elisabeth off.

"Can you forgive me?" Elisabeth asked before leaving.

Mammi nodded again, and Elisabeth knew Mammi wasn't going to do or say any more than that. She continued into the front room.

Elisabeth placed Anna's skirts on her bed, laying each one out separately. Then she scurried through the kitchen again to get everyone's blouses and the women's *tschuraks* —light, fitted, formal jackets that cinched at the waist before expanding several centimetres over the skirts and apron.

Two hours later, with supper just being set, Elisabeth found herself standing in front of the looking glass in the front room, her four underskirts and outer skirt already tied on, and her blouse tucked in. Her hair hung in waves to below her waist; it had become messy from all the running around, so she needed to redo it. Everyone else was ready, but she wasn't going to show her face to her mother with hair that looked like it had been through the biblical Flood.

"Can I do it?" Anna asked as she entered the room.

"You may braid it, but I'll pin it," Elisabeth replied.

Rosina and Mammi were busy setting out the last

embroidered tablecloths, cushions, and table runners in the back room for tomorrow's afternoon dinner while Luki was given the Bible and told to practise his reading. Most of the food was finally prepared, ready to be cooked up the following day. Only the potatoes were left because they would turn grey if they weren't cooked soon after being cut.

Anna pulled over a chair and stood on it, and Elisabeth handed her a brush. As Anna pulled the brush through Elisabeth's blonde hair, Elisabeth couldn't help but wonder how her younger siblings felt now that Tata was gone. With all the time spent preparing for Christmas Eve and Christmas Day, they had never spoken about it. She asked Anna now.

"I miss him a lot," Anna replied, but said nothing further. She handed the brush back to Elisabeth and then pulled the sides of Elisabeth's hair to the back and began to braid.

"But you've never said anything," Elisabeth remarked.

"I don't want to get in trouble like you."

Elisabeth could feel Anna tug lightly as she braided her hair. Truth be told, she loved it when one of her sisters did her hair because of the gentle tickling feeling on her scalp.

"I won't get you in trouble," Elisabeth said. "You can talk to me about it."

Anna stepped down from the chair now that the braid was getting longer, pushed the chair out of the way, and stood directly behind Elisabeth, but not before Elisabeth caught a glimpse of her sister's eyes in the looking glass: they were turning red. Elisabeth regretted raising the topic right before the family sat down for a modest Christmas Eve dinner.

"Listen, Anna. I don't want to make you sad on Christmas Eve. We can talk about Tata together when we miss him."

Anna finished the braid and passed its end to Elisabeth.

"If I talk to Jesus, then no one will know and I won't get into trouble," Anna said.

Elisabeth had to smile: a logical answer to an emotional problem, exactly what she would expect from Anna.

"Well, if you need someone who answers you back in a way that you can hear, you can talk to me. Now, you'd better get going. No need for both of us to be late to the table."

Anna left, and Elisabeth folded the braid to the top of her head, stuck a comb in against it, and then inserted hairpins to keep it all in place.

After one last glance in the looking glass, she headed into the kitchen to join her family.

CHAPTER ELEVEN

"Oh, there you are!" Uncle Peter called across the kitchen, flashing a big grin as Juliana entered. Every picture Juliana had ever seen of Uncle Peter, right down to some of him in his teens in one of Mom's old photo albums, showed him with that grin. She'd never met him before, but Juliana couldn't help but smile back at him.

"Does he always smile like that?" Juliana whispered to Sophie.

"Yup. Best to get used to it. But he's the cool Schuhmacher sibling."

Juliana snorted.

Mom called Juliana over to the stove and passed her a pot to carry to the table. So far so good. If all Mom needed help with was carrying things, Juliana could do it. It wasn't fun, but it wasn't horrid. Carrying things was neutral.

The normally round kitchen table that was barely big enough for four had been lengthened with an insert and extended by adding a small table Dad had carried up from the laundry room earlier. A bunch of old wooden chairs had been brought in from the garage, and when Juliana placed the pot on a hot plate on the table, she bumped one of them and it rocked sideways. She made a mental note not to sit on that chair.

"Juliana, can you quickly wash that head of lettuce?"

Really? Was her mom trying to torture her? Juliana huffed and headed for the kitchen sink. "Fine."

"I think the salad spinner is in here," said Rebecca, bending to rummage through dishes stacked in a cupboard in the wall unit.

"How are your studies going?" Dad asked her, clearly ignoring Juliana. "I hear you've started your master's in mathematics now?"

Rebecca handed an old, orange salad spinner to Juliana and nodded. "I love it: it's really challenging. I'm just glad I finished this semester. But I still have five more to go."

Juliana stared at the massive head of romaine lettuce in the sink. Now? On Christmas Eve? Her parents knew she *hated* this kitchen task above all others.

Mom leaned over to her. "We're eating in thirty

minutes. All the other vegetables for the salad are done, thanks to your Aunt Anne."

"Dad could've done this," Juliana replied.

"Your dad's still recovering from all that driving."

Juliana glanced over at Dad, who was laughing at something someone said. *Yeah, definitely recovering.*

"Then why doesn't your brother help you."

Mom sighed. "We live here now. Annie's showing me where everything is and what appliances have 'a personality.' But otherwise, we're cooking. End of discussion."

Juliana removed the strainer from the spinner bowl, set it on the counter, and waited for the bowl to fill with cold water. Of all the tasks Mom could've asked help for. One by one, Juliana ripped each outer leaf off. She could hear her mom sigh at Juliana's slow pace.

"Does Opa have a green cart?" Juliana asked.

"The green bin's over there." Mom pointed to a brown bin tucked back in the corner of the counter.

She couldn't even get the name of the local composting program right without being corrected. Letting out a heavy sigh, Juliana continued washing and ripping. She remembered how Rachel had laughed when she had found out how long it took Juliana to rip lettuce.

"Just do it and be done with it," she'd said.

"I hate it," Juliana had replied. "And if I go slow enough, Mom will stop asking me to do it someday."

Rachel had reacted the same way Sophie had in Juliana's bedroom just minutes before. She had to admit,

Sophie laughing was funny in itself. *Glad I provided some humour*, she thought. Other friends had asked why she wasn't allowed to cut the lettuce with a knife.

"Because lettuce rusts faster," Mom had said on more than one occasion.

Showing Mom that the Internet had a different opinion hadn't helped.

Opa came up behind Juliana and patted her on the back. "Did you know that your oma always ripped lettuce, too? That way it looked like we had servants." He laughed his good-natured laugh and walked into the living room.

Juliana certainly felt like one. Ready-to-serve lettuce existed for a reason: so you didn't have to waste time ripping it.

Seriously, Juliana thought. *If everyone wants to sit around and chat, why not just buy everything, dump it in serving bowls, and sit down and eat? What's the point of cooking anymore?* She looked around. *And the men really can't help?*

She understood why Opa didn't cook, but Dad, Uncle Peter, Uncle Phillip, and her three male cousins?

When she finished, she said so and immediately returned to her room to avoid being asked to help with any other kitchen work. It was Christmas Eve. It'd be nice if her parents showed her *some* understanding.

She dropped onto her sleeping bag. Only three more days until she'd have Internet and a SIM card again.

But only moments later, she heard from the hallway, "Where's my Yulika?"

"Moping in her room," Dad said.

Juliana hated the paper-thin walls. Her eyes welled up.

"We are a big family," Opa said. "This is very new for her. She has no brothers and sisters."

"No," Juliana said to herself. "But I had lots of friends. They meant the same to me."

The hallway floor creaked as Opa walked down it, and Juliana was scared he'd open up her door and come in. The last thing she needed was another speech from an adult.

To be fair, he wasn't the reason for her anger. If anything, he'd been nice to her this entire time, even patient with her, though she had heard him yell at Mom that morning, something about getting lunchtime meals delivered, which he didn't want because he found it too… something. He'd switched to German by then. To her surprise, her mother had begun inserting German words into the conversation. But Juliana still got the gist: "She was telling him what to do, too," Juliana said out loud.

She double-tapped on a photo from her first class back after the summer's last dance competition. She, Declan, Rachel, Matilda, Linda, and the rest of the competition team were posed in front of the competition's big sign, their purple-and-gold studio warm-up suits on, hair back in curled ponytails (except for Declan's), faces made up (except for Declan's) with bright red lipstick, pink blush, heavy eyeliner, and purple eyeshadow to match the tap-line costumes they were about to change into.

"All thirty of us don't even smile enough to equal Uncle Peter's smile." She giggled at her own remark. Her uncle did seem really friendly, too, like Opa, but in a dorky way, as opposed to a grandfatherly way. He had a mullet to go with the huge grin.

Her door slammed open and Juliana jumped. Both her parents now stood at the foot of her sleeping bag. She had never seen them this angry.

"What is wrong with you?" Dad asked. "You have an entire loving family out there who wants to meet you, and you're hiding here in your room, sulking like a little kid."

Juliana was scared she'd start to cry if she said anything.

"Well?" Mom asked. "You just disappeared. You owe us an explanation."

Juliana stared at her phone, praying that her parents would leave her alone if she just ignored them. Instead, Dad ripped her phone out of her hands.

"Why the attitude, Juliana Elizabeth?"

The middle name. Juliana knew she was in trouble. She remained silent.

"You're not the only one going through a transition here," Mom said.

Juliana couldn't hold it inside anymore. "But I was the only one *forced* into this transition, and I'm the only one who hardly knows anyone!" she shouted. "I have no friends. This is not my bedroom. This is not my home!"

Dad's face tightened up, the way it always did when he

got angry, and he sighed. The angry sigh. "You're the one whose attitude is affecting everyone else."

"Then just leave me alone and go on with your little Christmas party!" Juliana jumped up, pushed past her parents, and stormed out of her room. She entered the kitchen and felt like she had stepped into a scene from a Hollywood movie, where everyone was frozen in place, glasses halfway to their mouths, and all eyes on the embarrassed main character.

"I'm sorry," she mumbled and ran down the stairs and straight ahead into the rec room. She slammed the door behind her and flicked on the light in time to see a cloud of dust rise from her entrance.

"Oh my god," she said, and then sneezed once, twice, three times. The rec room looked like it had never been cleaned. Cream-coloured wallpaper was peeling off all around the room. Cobwebs hung from the ceiling, and fly carcasses were trapped in ancient webs strung between metal bars on the windows. The furniture was brown and orange and covered in dust. To her left was another door and beside it a drink bar with orange vinyl with black dots across the front.

She sneezed again and wiped her nose on the back of her hand. The door to her left stood partway open, and Juliana didn't know if she should peek inside or stay where she was. All she knew was that she couldn't go back upstairs, but she shuddered at the thought of sitting on that furniture. What was she going to do? Stand in one place?

She tiptoed through the dust-laden shag carpet, its polyester fibres scratching at her bare feet. She gripped the door handle and paused. What if a dead animal was back there? Didn't Mom say her parents used to have cats? When had the last one died? She didn't see a light switch on the wall, so she'd have to open the door all the way to see anything inside.

Juliana held her breath as the door squeaked on its hinges. Ahead, she saw a lightbulb with a chain hanging from it. She lowered her gaze to the cement floor to look for anything gross. Seeing only dust, she stepped in on demi-pointe, the cold of the floor travelling through the balls of her bare feet and up her legs and into her core. She reached for the chain, closed her eyes, and pulled.

CHAPTER TWELVE

lisabeth closed her eyes and prayed to Jesus that He help her through Christmas Eve without her father. She opened them, pulled her own shawl tightly around her, and brushed a few pieces of lint from Luki's coat sleeves. In the absence of the church bells, some neighbours rang cowbells, but for Elisabeth, the higher-pitched, frantic ringing of the smaller bells couldn't replace the loud clanging of the big and small church bells that announced it was almost time for evening service.

Elisabeth's duty was to help the other children dress and get them out the door so Mammi could set up the Christmas tree on the table in the front room.

It was as though Tata was away at war again.

"Do you know your prayers off by heart?" Elisabeth

asked. "You must be ready for when the *Christkind* and *stornickels* come."

Luki and Anna nodded, but Rosina looked nervous.

"I was busy helping! I forgot to practise!" she said.

Elisabeth gave her sister a stern look, the kind of look she'd expect Mammi to give them. "You can pray while you clean, Rosina," she said.

"But that's hard!" Rosina protested.

Elisabeth waved her siblings toward the street, mindful to keep their gaze away from the front windows so they wouldn't catch Mammi setting up the tree. She wanted them to be as surprised as she used to be when she was their age and didn't know that the parents were the ones responsible for this touch of Christmas magic.

As Elisabeth led them down their property to the front gate, she tried to think of something to keep the kids' minds off their mother. While Tata was in the war, they had sung Christmas carols. Worried that reliving those years again would cause her to cry, she thought of something else.

"Then let's help Rosina and practise our prayers," she suggested. "That way you're all ready for the *stornickels*. You know they'll give you a piece of coal when they visit us tonight if you can't say your prayers."

"I know my prayers," Luki said.

Anna nodded in agreement.

"Prayers are boring," Rosina added.

"Rosina! Hold your tongue!" Elisabeth scolded.

"And when Tata was in the war," Anna said, "we sang carols on the way to church to make us happy. We should do that again."

A logical answer. Of course. Only… Elisabeth didn't know if she could pretend like Tata was with them.

"But prayers are something different," she countered.

"Can't we sing?" Luki asked.

"And where's Mammi?" Rosina asked. She looked toward the house, and Elisabeth jumped in her way.

"Fine," Elisabeth said. "We can sing. What will we sing?"

"'Silent Night'! 'Silent Night'!" Rosina shouted.

How could Rosina remember what they had sung in those years? Elisabeth felt a lump forming in her throat, but she started the carol. By the time they'd finished the second verse, they had rounded the corner, and Elisabeth was fighting hard to hold back tears. She had promised to be a better daughter to Mammi. *Mammi didn't cry in front of the children, and neither will I*, Elisabeth thought.

The closer they got to the church, the more friends and acquaintances they saw, and the easier it became for Elisabeth to take her mind off her father. Rosina wanted to run off to see a friend, but Elisabeth grabbed her by the collar of her *tschurak* and kept her with the family. At the stairs to the church stood Pastor Fröhlich, his usual black robes covered in a black coat. He was ringing a hand bell and greeting everyone as they entered. Mammi came rushing up behind them.

Dressed in her black Sunday attire, Mammi's black outer skirt puffed out in a beautiful, smooth circle over her underskirts. Her blouse was hidden under her black *tschurak*. Her navy-blue apron, which Elisabeth had pressed herself, hung effortlessly against all the black. And on her head, Mammi wore a stiffened, black kerchief that tied under her chin and hung down to the base of her neck in the back. Elisabeth couldn't wait to wear clothes like that after she got married and had a family someday.

"What did you forget?" Luki asked her.

"What do you mean?"

Elisabeth gave Mammi a knowing look. "I told them you'd forgotten something and that's why we left ahead of you."

"Ah, yes, of course," Mammi said, somewhat too unnaturally for Elisabeth's liking, though the other children didn't seem to notice. "Just my handkerchiefs. But no more chit-chat now. We're at church."

Pastor Fröhlich wished each family member a Merry Christmas as they passed by him and through the main door.

The smell of burning candles greeted Elisabeth's nose. Their simple church, with its two columns of pews, small pulpit, and high nave on the ground level, and its organ and balcony above, was lit with hundreds of candles.

Pastor Fröhlich always preached that the light of Jesus was everywhere, and at Christmastime, Elisabeth believed it. A helper passed Elisabeth and each family member a small candle in a glass holder and Elisabeth felt like she was holding Jesus in her hands as she guided her siblings up to the balcony, where all children who hadn't been confirmed sat. From up there, she watched the adults below separate themselves: the men to the left and the women to the right, with confirmed but unmarried young adults—like Maria—sitting up near the pastor in a special spot. It didn't take long for Mammi to disappear into the crowd of similarly dressed women: all women past a certain age wore black formal clothing.

The organist, sitting at the small pipe organ on the balcony with the children, played quietly as everyone entered. Elisabeth for a moment took in her family. Anna and Rosina, in their white kerchiefs, couldn't have looked more angelic as they, too, stared in awe at all the candles in the church. Luki wrinkled his nose. He never liked the smell of so many burning candles.

Everyone looked like they got along with one another, which wasn't always the case. Elisabeth thought back to a discussion that happened in the churchyard last Sunday, after service, when Frau Krehling had begun discussing with Mammi why Pastor Fröhlich wouldn't allow the congregation to join the synod in Siebenbürgen, a large area in Romania's Carpathian Mountains. The Siebenbürgen Sachsens were another German group, with a different history than the Germans in the Banat. That's what Tata had told Elisabeth, anyway.

Frau Müller agreed that it seemed silly to continue belonging to the synod in Hungary, especially because, according to her husband, it was now required that official church business be recorded in Hungarian instead of German.

"Belonging to the Klausenburg synod in Siebenbürgen would have meant we could continue to use German for official church business."

"However," Mammi had said, "my husband said that the churches we made our song book with are part of the Hungarian synod. They are our community."

Elisabeth had wanted to join in the conversation several times, but each time, all three women had given her mean looks and continued talking, as though she hadn't existed. But if Elisabeth had left the group, Mammi would have gotten angry at her for being rude: she was too old to run around and play with the children.

Then why am I sitting up here with my siblings? she thought as she continued to listen to the lovely organ music. She knew why: she was not yet confirmed and therefore also not married.

The organist stopped, the silence signalling to those below that Christmas Eve service was about to begin. He then played the opening notes to "Oh, How Joyfully" and everyone stood. As each note rang through the candle-lit stillness that engulfed the church, they unveiled to Elisabeth the miracle of Jesus's birth. A shiver ran through her spine.

No one needed to open their hymnals; they all knew the words by heart:

Oh, how joyfully; oh, how merrily

Christmas comes with its grace divine.

Grace again is beaming; Christ the world redeeming.

Hail, ye Christians, hail the joyous Christmastime!

With the harmonious melodies of their modest pipe organ, and the voices singing, Elisabeth was certain she could feel Jesus entering her heart. Did Tata feel the same?

LUKI AND ROSINA couldn't get their boots off fast enough. Mammi even slapped Rosina on the cheek for dropping her shawl on the floor instead of carrying it to the back room, folding it, and laying it in a drawer in the wardrobe.

"I made that shawl for Elisabeth and it has been passed down to Anna and now you. You show respect to your family by taking care of the gifts they have given you," she admonished her youngest child.

Rosina, crying from being reprimanded, but Luki and Anna laughing in anticipation of what was about to come, the three siblings ran into the front room. Elisabeth took

Mammi's shawl and hers, folded them, and lay them on top of those of her sisters, then walked back through the kitchen and into the front room, almost skipping as she went.

The Christmas tree was perhaps one-and-a-half metres tall, a majestic height, and it stood on the table in the middle of the front room. Several paper ornaments hung on it. Mammi opened a box of matches, struck a match, and lit the candles perched on the tree. Their gentle light reminded Elisabeth yet again why they were celebrating this evening. Small packages were laid around the tree's base.

"Elisabeth, go make the tea. The water is already in the pot on the kitchen table," Mammi instructed. "Anna, you may get a tray of cookies."

Anna jumped in the air and clapped her hands. Too young to remember much of life before the war, Anna had grown up in a time when cookies only came out at Christmas, Easter, christenings, and funerals. Elisabeth, though, remembered an earlier time, when cookies came out every Sunday to entertain any families who dropped by to visit.

Elisabeth placed the pot on the stove, fed the oven another bushel of cornstalks that had been brought in this afternoon, and closed the pot with a lid, all while Luki begged her to hurry up. She glanced up at the crucifix over the house door and again prayed, this time asking for patience.

"Come on, Elisabeth!"

She took a breath before answering. "Luki, it takes time to boil the water." She pulled out six teacups from the cupboard at the other end of the kitchen. Only after she set the teacups down did she notice she'd miscounted: she only needed five. Her heart ached as she placed one teacup back and grabbed the canister of dried chamomile flowers.

"Elisabeth!" Luki whined.

"Stop it!" she yelled back at her brother. *Why do my angry words come out so fast?* she thought, again regretting her reaction.

Mammi shouted from behind the Christmas tree. "Show your brother some patience: he's six years younger than you!"

Elisabeth clenched her jaw and sighed.

"Don't you have something to say?" Mammi asked.

Elisabeth sighed again. "I'm sorry," she murmured.

"And?" Mammi prodded.

Her cheeks burned as the question rose from her throat. "Will you forgive me, Luki?"

"I'll think about it," came the response. Elisabeth heard a swat and Luki began to cry.

Elisabeth wished she had someone to talk to about all this. Praying to Jesus helped, but it wasn't the same as talking to someone. Her father, for example. Or Maria.

Or was there a way she could maybe draw what she was thinking? She loved to draw. Then she could show Tata when he came home what she had been thinking.

No. Mammi would never allow it. She'd say I was wasting my time.

Elisabeth sighed and prayed to Jesus to make the water boil faster.

Apparently He was listening to someone else's prayers this evening.

CHAPTER THIRTEEN

*J*uliana peeked through barely open eyes the way a child did after a jack-in-the-box had frightened them. Still standing on demi-pointe and holding the chain, she looked around.

The lightbulb shone an eerie yellow hue Juliana had only seen in old movies. In front of her was an old green fridge with the doors taken off but its shelves stacked with old dishes, small kitchen appliances, and folded fabric that looked like Miss Kasia could've used it for a number from the seventies. Two tall wooden shelves stood next to it, filled with empty mason jars and a box containing all the lids. As she turned her head to the right, she saw boxes upon boxes piled up against the wall, many with their flaps open. She let go of the chain and lowered her heels. She crept over to the boxes, sneezed again, and lifted the flap of a box that almost seemed to teeter at the top of the pile, like a boulder nearing its tipping point.

In the box lay numerous leather-bound books with gold-embossed writing and decorations on brown spines. The script was fancy, like something out of an old movie. She wiped her nose, reached into the box, and pulled out a book. Its cover was navy blue and had no title, just little black triangles at the top and bottom right-hand corners. She inspected the spine again. The script of the title was too elaborate for her to make out the letters, but below the title was an embossed creature of some kind: it had a lion's body and tail, a hawk's wings, and a bird's face. One paw rested on some kind of shield that had more elaborate letters and the number *1805*. The shield itself rested on two books. Below the image was the number *16*, then more letters.

The book's binding cracked as she gently opened the cover. Juliana felt like her eyes were crossing as she stared at the ornate script. She blinked, partly hoping her eyes would somehow figure out the strange letters and partly because they were beginning to itch from all the dust. A sneeze formed again in her nose and she turned her head just in time to miss the book and instead blow more dust into the air.

She looked back at the title page.

"That looks like 'conversations' but with a *k*," she said to herself. The word above started with *B...r...o...c...*

maybe a lowercase *b*? The last letter was an *d*. But was that an *n* or a *u* before the *d*?

She turned the page and saw more illegible writing. However, at the bottom in clear type was *1889*.

If that was a date—she paused for a moment as she did the math in her head—this book was over one hundred and twenty-five years old. No wonder its condition was this bad. She paged through a little. Near the middle she found something folded up but attached to the book. She opened it to reveal a world map, printed in colour. At the top, in regular font, it said,

ÜBERSICHTSKARTE DES WELTVERKEHRS.

"I could really use Internet access right now," she said to herself.

Canada was in its normal spot at the top left of the map. Across its expanse were the words "BRIT. NORD-AMERIKA." Through all of the world's oceans were curved lines connecting the continents. She held the book right under the lightbulb so she could better see the tiny print along each of the lines: "Rotterdam—N. York," "Liverpool—Halifax," and "Liverp—Para—Ceará" were just a few.

"I guess this is where ships travelled."

She folded up the map, closed the book, and slid it back into the box. Her curiosity piqued, she gingerly opened another box.

"Ahh!" she cried out and jumped back. Several dried-up insect carcasses lay on top of one of the books. She aimed her mouth in their direction, closed her eyes, and blew, trying really hard to ignore the sound of their shells hitting the side of the box. When she opened her eyes again, the bugs were gone.

The cover of that book looked identical to the one she'd just opened. In fact, all the books in the box seemed to be identical except for the number and combination of letters at the bottom.

"Like that encyclopedia set Mrs. Palubeski showed us back in grade seven," she said. But, for the life of her, Juliana couldn't make out the words on the spines.

The old-fashioned script reminded her of tap: to anyone who didn't study it, tap looked like a bunch of blurred movements making crisp sounds. But to anyone who knew tap, each step had a name, a sound, and a volume level, and together, they worked like letters, making up words and then stories, depending on how they were combined. If she could read these letters, she could type them into an online translator and figure out what the book said.

"Like that'll happen anytime soon," she said. Even if she had Internet, with their belongings finally arriving in a few days, she'd be busy with getting organized again until school started.

She moved the box of encyclopedias out of the way so she could inspect more boxes.

Now I feel like a real snoop, she thought, but she couldn't help herself. The next box had more modern books, and as she lifted them out, she saw that many had to do with a hostage situation in Iran. Their paper covers were sometimes torn, sometimes not, but they interested her less than that old encyclopedia set. As she was about to place the books back into the box, she saw another leather-bound book. This one was smaller than the encyclopedias, much smaller, and had no writing on the spine. Juliana pulled it out and opened it. Another dead bug welcomed her, its legs crinkled against its body. She almost dropped the book, but her fingers seemed to understand and held on to it as though it was something precious. So blew the bug away instead.

The first page was written in handwriting, but again she couldn't make out what it said. Needing better light, she left the cellar and sneezed again from the dust in the rec room. Opa's room would certainly have more light and less dust, so she headed there. Now feeling like a complete intruder, she flicked on the light and went in.

Opa's room was small, with more of that shag carpeting, but the carpet had clearly been visited by a vacuum. The same peeling wallpaper from the rec room covered the walls in Opa's room, and he only had one tiny window with bars in front of it for light. What were the bars for?

A single bed made of dark wood lay against the wall. A doily covered the surface of the night table. Juliana fingered it and guessed it was made of yarn or something similar. Along the opposite wall was a wardrobe with large doors for anything Opa needed to hang up, and a chest for anything that could be stored folded. Both matched the bed and the night table.

I hope he doesn't get angry at me, she thought as she sat on his neatly made bed. She placed the book on the bedspread and, barely touching it, opened the cover and then turned to the page after the handwriting. There she saw a pencil drawing, somewhat smudged, of a room.

The artist had apparently stood in a corner and looked into the room. In the middle of the page, but higher up, was a doorway with a *t* hanging above it.

That's probably a cross, Juliana thought. The Roths weren't religious, but her mom had explained that she'd grown up Lutheran, a form of Christianity, so Juliana knew the basics.

Through the door could be seen part of a window on the far wall. In the foreground and to the right were part of a table and a few chairs, shaded to look like they were made of wood. To the left, next to that doorway, she saw a cube of some kind sticking out of the wall, but she couldn't figure out what it was. It had a darkened door in the middle of it. A table stood next to it with long sticks of some kind in a basket.

Juliana carefully flipped through one page after another. Had Opa drawn them? But Mom had never mentioned that Opa drew. At the same time, Mom had rarely said anything about her family's history. Would Opa be angry if Juliana took the book into her room to look at it some more?

Scratching sounds from above signalled that everyone was sitting down to eat supper.

"Great," she said. She'd put the book back for now; the last thing she wanted was to have everyone see her with it, especially if she wasn't supposed to be rummaging in the cellar to begin with.

She stood up and smoothed out the bed first. She'd be sure to tell Opa that she had gone in there, but later, when she had time to talk to him alone. The *really* last thing she needed was Mom and Dad lecturing her again.

She turned off the light and tiptoed back into the rec room.

"Oh, god," she said as she noticed even more dust and cobwebs than she had seen the first time. The ceiling vent caught her attention, and she noticed it was closed. *Opening that should help with the air down here,* she thought. She reached up and pushed hard with her thumb against the tiny lever in the vent to open it. A dead spider fell out when the flaps shifted and she shrieked and danced as though she were on hot coals.

"Oh my god, oh my god, oh my god! Where'd it go?" She danced as she inspected her dress and the floor. She didn't know what she'd dread more: not finding the spider and therefore not knowing where it was, or finding it on herself. She'd have to check herself over in Opa's bathroom.

She tiptoed over the scratchy carpet to the cellar to return the collection of drawings.

Was that cookies she could now smell coming from upstairs? But a loud, shrill sound startled her and she jumped, almost dropping the book. She heard the ringing again: it was Opa's phone. She put the book on a box.

"Juliana!" Dad called down the stairs. "Rachel's on the phone!"

CHAPTER FOURTEEN

The butter cookies Elisabeth had baked were passed around on an heirloom silver platter. She had cut the dough into stars, hearts, and Christmas trees with cookie cutters, and later had decorated them with icing made from icing sugar and water, squeezing out the most exquisite patterns from a piping bag she had sewn herself last year. She bit into one now and let it melt in her mouth, while her sisters and brother shovelled cookies into their mouths so fast that Mammi ripped the platter out of their hands and lectured them about the seven deadly sins.

The chamomile tea wasn't black tea, but at least it was warm. It reminded her a little too much of flus and stomach pains, but she drank it anyway.

Once everyone had had a sip of tea and several cookies, Mammi passed out the gifts. First came the oranges—

the only time in the whole year that the children got to eat one. Rosina almost broke her nose as she pressed it against her orange to smell its sweet scent. Anna rubbed her hands all over hers and then sniffed them. Luki licked his orange and his face squished into a raisin.

Elisabeth giggled. "You have to cut it open before you eat it." They only received one orange a year. It was natural that someone as young as Luki would have forgotten how to eat it.

Mammi then passed around four small packages wrapped in brown paper. Elisabeth's felt like a book, and her heart began to race. The past few Christmases, they had usually received either embroidered handkerchiefs or new mittens.

Rosina began to tear at hers and Mammi admonished her for being so greedy. Rosina sulked after the punishment was doled out: she had to wait until last to finish opening hers.

Anna gingerly opened hers and gave a little yelp. "My own pair of mittens!" she cried out. Elisabeth was happy for her sister, who always had to wear Elisabeth's old clothes. To add to the difficulties, Elisabeth preferred pink, but Anna liked red.

Luki opened his package next. "A man's pair of mittens! Black! Just like Tata's gloves!" he said. Instead of the brightly coloured hand-me-down mittens he'd had to wear from Anna (and therefore from Elisabeth), he now had a pair of his very own black ones.

A knock at the door interrupted the gift giving. Mammi stood up, brushed the crumbs off her apron, and answered. The younger children all ran up behind her, knowing exactly who it was going to be.

Standing outside the door were several older children dressed in costume. The *Christkind* wore a white dress and carried in her arms a little baby doll. Next to her stood another girl about Elisabeth's age, dressed in a white gown and holding a whip made of twine. Three other children were dressed as *stornickels*, wearing oversized felt caps and masks with fringe hanging around the long horns that protruded from the top. Luki and Rosina charged back into the front room and hid behind the table and tree.

"Can the *Christkind* come in?" the older children asked.

"Yes." Mammi smiled slightly and stood back from the door, welcoming them in. Elisabeth immediately recognized them as former classmates but knew that it was her job now to keep their secret.

The *Christkind* group stood inside the door so Mammi could close it.

"Lukas," one of the *stornickels* called in a gruff voice.

"Anna," called another.

"Rosina," called the third.

One by one, the young children crept back out into the kitchen and faced the kindly smiles of the *Christkind*, the harsh expression of the angel with her whip, and the non-human faces of the three *stornickels*.

"Can you say a prayer for me?" the *Christkind* asked,

and all three nodded, though Elisabeth noticed beads of sweat forming on Rosina's temples. Luki and Anna began and Rosina joined in, watching their lips and listening to every word, always a half-word behind them. She wrung her hands, her eyes shifting between the angel's whip and the three *stornickels* when she finished. Only when they *all* received each two walnuts did Rosina relax. Everyone wished each other a Merry Christmas, and the *Christkind* group moved on to the next home with little children. Rosina beamed.

Elisabeth gave her siblings a hug, and Mammi gave them an approving nod.

"Can we get back to our gifts?" Elisabeth asked eagerly. The moment she finished the question, though, she knew she shouldn't have asked it.

"Elisabeth," Mammi scolded. "Did Maria or Josef ask for their gifts?"

Sheepishly, Elisabeth shook her head.

"You can wait until tomorrow morning now."

Elisabeth glared at Mammi. "That's not fair! Tata's—"

"You're not the only one who misses your father," Mammi retorted, "and yet the rest of us are coping fine."

An uncomfortable silence fell over the family as everyone walked back into the front room. Elisabeth was boiling mad. How little did Mammi know about her own children? But if Elisabeth shared what Anna had told her, she'd be betraying her sister's trust. She couldn't do that.

Once they all took their seats, Rosina spoke up.

"Mammi, it is Christmas Eve. Jesus says we should forgive."

Mammi's eyes widened in anger. "You can both wait until tomorrow. I will not be told by my children how they should be raised." She stood up and took the platter of cookies into the kitchen.

Rosina began to cry.

"That is enough!" Mammi shouted.

Elisabeth knew their mother would hit her sister as soon as Mammi returned to the front room.

"I know it's cold outside, but go fetch us some corn-stalks so the oven stays warm just a little longer tonight."

Rosina nodded, and Elisabeth followed her sister to the house door in the kitchen, being sure to stay between her and Mammi the whole time.

Why did adults tell children to follow Jesus' teachings, like being nice to one another, but they could be mean when they wanted to? So far as Elisabeth knew, Jesus didn't hit when He was angry.

"CHILDREN, obey your parents in the Lord; for this is right. Honour thy father and mother; which is the first commandment with promise: that it may be well with thee, and thou mayest live long on the earth." Elisabeth paused. She tried to make her mouth moist, but after whispering Ephesians 6: 1-3 many times, her mouth had dried out.

What she really needed was water, but that would mean going into the kitchen to find some.

The entire family lay asleep in their beds in the front room. It was pitch black. Mammi snored. Anna made hardly a sound. Rosina mumbled now and then. Luki barely lay still for long, leaving Elisabeth to wonder whether he was actually asleep.

All Elisabeth could do was lay there and try to figure out why she couldn't behave the way Jesus asked her to. She had only wanted a moment of joy, to see what she would get, and she couldn't keep quiet. Tomorrow was the happiest day of the year after Christmas Eve, a day when her mother's siblings and their families would come by, and Elisabeth was still thinking about her present.

Elisabeth sat up. Her bed was opposite the door to the kitchen, next to one of the windows facing the street, so reaching the kitchen meant navigating around the other furniture. She pulled a blanket over her shoulders—the oven had also fallen into its cold nighttime slumber by now —and tiptoed through the room.

"Owa!"

She managed to keep her voice down but her knee had bumped a chair and pushed it into the table. Mammi stopped snoring and Elisabeth stood perfectly still. Within a few moments, though, Mammi's snoring began again, and Elisabeth felt her way around the table and chairs. She reached out one arm and worked her way toward the door, one small step after another. She overshot her angle and touched the protruding back side of the oven, but now she knew she was close. She felt along the oven to the wall, and then found the handle and opened the door.

Once in the kitchen, she breathed a sigh of relief. The moon shone through the single window, making it easy for her to find a lantern and a box of matches.

Holding the lit lantern ahead of her, she immediately saw her gift sitting square in the middle of the kitchen table, calling to her to open it. She set the lantern on the table and sat down. Her thirst could wait.

She reached out a hand to touch the gift but she yanked it back. Wasn't it moments like these that Martin Luther always spoke of? Ones where the devil was trying his hand? She had to fight it.

But she only received one big gift a year, and this one was by far the largest: perhaps ten or twelve centimetres wide by twenty-five centimetres or so tall. She knew it was at least a book. But what kind of book? Surely not a drawing book: her mother wouldn't let her father pay for another one. Elisabeth was certain of that. There was also something of the same shape under the book and then three long bumps under that.

Elisabeth reached out for it again.

"No, I mustn't." She abruptly stood up.

She picked up the lantern, then searched for a jug of drinking water and found it on the washing table in the far right corner. A few scoops into her mouth quenched her thirst. She dared not return to the kitchen table so she headed into the back room. Maybe some reading would take her mind off her temptation. She pulled down a book of Martin Luther's sermons that she always read when she felt her soul needed help.

The back room's dirt floor was covered in large woven carpets, while the sofa and benches were draped in the Schuhmachers' best crocheted blankets. A table runner that had been crocheted by Elisabeth's great-grandmother, one of the original Lutheran settlers in Semlak, lay across the dining table, and one embroidered serviette lay folded on each placemat. The guest bed was piled high with pillows and blankets.

Elisabeth was scared she might mess up the hand-somely decorated room, but if she took the book into the kitchen, she risked getting it dirty, the punishment for which would likely be more severe.

She set the lantern down at the edge of the dining table and placed the book next to it, careful not to disturb the table setting. She searched for the sermon she preferred in times of temptation: "Our Conduct Toward God: Rejoice in Him."

She whispered as she read, making Luther's words feel more real than if she just read them silently. After she finished the first page, she turned it and continued reading. Then, one passage jumped out at her:

Hence the expression, "Rejoice in the Lord"; not rejoice in silver or gold, not in eating or drinking, not in pleasure or mechanical chanting, not in strength or health, not in skill or wisdom, not in power or honour, not in friendship or favour, nay, not in good works or holiness even. For these are deceptive joys, false joys, which never stir the depths of the heart. They are never even felt.

Elisabeth glanced out into the kitchen. Was she rejoicing in her gift instead of in God? She continued reading. Another passage of Luther's, this time something the apostle Paul wrote, stood out to her:

The apostle further commands in our text to rejoice "always." Thus he rebukes those who rejoice in God—who praise and thank him—only a portion of the time. These rejoice when it is well with them; when not, rejoicing ceases.

Which is what I've been doing because of Tata's departure, she thought. *I've only been rejoicing when things go well for me. If I keep rejoicing in God, then I'll stop worrying about the gift.*

Surviving the war had been hard on everyone: food had become scarce, families had lost their husbands, fathers, and sons, and now with her village's move to Romania, everyone was nervous about their future. It had been hard to keep her faith in God during those times, but she had managed to do so.

"And I'm worrying about a Christmas gift," Elisabeth said to herself. Moreover, Elisabeth knew from her confirmation studies that the fourth commandment was to honour her parents. She needed to listen to Mammi and not open that gift.

She glanced out to the kitchen table. On the other hand, Elisabeth was tired of being told what to do. Drawing always made her feel better. What if that gift was a new drawing book? Tata was usually the one to tell Mammi what to do. So he might have bought Elisabeth a new drawing book. She would certainly find it easier to cope with Tata's absence if she could draw about it.

But Mammi would never understand that, anyway. Mammi coped by drawing her lips into a thin line and moving on, something Elisabeth didn't believe she could do. If she couldn't draw, then she needed to talk to someone, but who?

CHAPTER FIFTEEN

"Where in God's name have you been?" Mom asked.

Juliana didn't appreciate the audience: everyone was indeed seated at the table, and now that Juliana was standing under full lights, she could see smudges on her shins and streaks of dust down her arms and across her beautiful red dress. Her cheeks turned almost the same colour.

"Never mind," Mom said. "Here." She handed Juliana the phone.

"Hello?" Juliana said.

"Hey, Juliana! It's Rachel! Merry Christmas! How are you doing?"

Juliana looked around and caught some stares and side glances. She chose to avoid the question so no one would hear her answer. "How'd you get my grandfather's number?" She moved around the corner and leaned against the wall. The cord stretched barely more than a metre.

"Your mom gave it to my mom. I did try calling you on WhatsApp earlier, but after I didn't hear from you, I asked Mom if there was another way to reach you."

"I have to hot spot to my parents' phones to get Internet, and they're not always available. Still no SIM card."

"Wow. That must suck."

"Yup."

"So? How's it going? How's your grandfather?"

Juliana tried to brush off some of the dust on her dress. "Fine," she said. She wanted to say more, but not in public like this.

"You okay?" Rachel asked.

"Sure."

Mom carried the bowl of salad to the table. Scott shouted, "I don't want salad tonight!"

"It's a bit loud," Rachel said. "Can you go somewhere else?"

"No. It's one of those old-fashioned phones. I'm attached to the wall."

"Ooooh. That's why you can't talk. Everyone can hear you."

"Mm-hmm."

"Can you Skype?"

"No Internet."

"Oh, man. That's gotta be brutal."

"Yup."

"That's why wireless access is a human right."

"Tell me about it."

Dean came over to Juliana and reached into her hair. Juliana was about to swat him away when she saw what he now held between his thumb and finger: the spider that had fallen out of the vent. Juliana squealed, jerking the receiver away and lifting the phone off its screw on the wall. It crashed on to the ground, its shrill ringer announcing its impact with the floor.

"Ask me next time first!"

"But you were on the phone!"

Opa shuffled over and patted her on the shoulder. "It's all right, Yulika," he said. "See if your friend is still there."

As Juliana lifted the receiver to her ear, he bent down, picked up the phone, and hung it back on its screw.

"Rachel?"

"Juliana? You still there?"

Juliana sighed. "Yeah."

"What happened?"

But all eyes were still on her. "Listen, can I call you later?"

"Um, sure." Rachel paused and then asked, "You're not okay, are you?"

Juliana brushed back the tears that had begun to form. "No."

"It's too much?"

"I hardly know them," she whispered, "and they're all staring at me."

Juliana tried not to pay attention to everyone in the room, but she could feel their gaze fixated on her like some kind of privacy-sucking vampires.

"Can you just all stop it!" she shouted. "I don't need you staring at me!"

"Juliana?" Rachel said. "Ignore them. What's going on?"

"Nothing. I'll call you back. Merry Christmas. Thanks for calling." Juliana hung up.

Her mother jumped out of her chair and stuck her face into Juliana's. "I've had it with this show. Everyone here is trying to enjoy Christmas, your best friend even called, I imagine to say she misses you and to see how you're doing, and you're acting like a self-absorbed little child."

Everything in Juliana was screaming that she needed to dance. Now. For her, dance was more than "just for fun." When things got tough at school—a hard test was coming up, she and a friend were having an argument—or at home—like when she missed her dad because of how long he was away—she could dance it out in the basement, where her practice studio was. It was her way of coping with the world. She couldn't just think her problems away like some people seemed to be able to. Of course, she'd talk to her friends, too, when she could, but dance was her private way of dealing with life. She might have even described it as spiritual.

And now, after not dancing for over a week, all the anger Juliana had bottled up exploded.

"Just leave me alone!"

Within a split second, she was down the stairs. She shot into the rec room, yanked the cellar door open, pulled on the light bulb chain, and slammed the door behind her. She didn't care anymore how many decomposing insects there were—it was better than being upstairs with all those staring strangers.

She reached for the journal and opened it to the first drawing again, the one of the empty kitchen. She could imagine herself sitting in there, all alone, with no strangers staring at her. Then at least she could talk to Rachel on the phone.

Even though she stood barefoot on the cold cement floor, her feet and whole body felt numb. Christmas couldn't get any worse than this.

"It's just not fair," she said, tears freely flowing. She really needed Rachel right now. The two had started at their Calgary dance studio the same year, had duets together, and even when they competed against each other in their solos, hugged each other regardless of who got the higher mark. When Rachel's parents had divorced, Juliana had spent many nights with Rachel as she cried about it. And Juliana's onstage accident? Rachel was the reason she returned to dance a better dancer.

Juliana wiped away her tears.

Sophie was really nice, but Juliana had just met her.

Sophie obviously didn't feel comfortable talking to Juliana about her challenges yet either, probably for the same reason, and that was okay. Their moms had tried to force them to become friends right away, and that had turned into an awkward situation. A new friendship wasn't the same as one that had been forged over ten years and through very challenging times.

"Maybe I should just get my phone and hot spot to Mom or Dad's," she said to herself. But her parents were livid with her now. They wouldn't let her use their phones until they'd "talked it out."

"Argh!" She stamped a foot on the floor. "I have no control over any of this!"

Juliana turned the page and stopped at another drawing.

"Beds, a couch, a table, chairs…all in the same room." But why? Surely someone would only draw what was important to them? "Oh…it's Christmas for this person, too." Juliana didn't recognize that at first because the small Christmas tree was perched in the middle of the table, like a very large houseplant. Candles stood on some of its sparse branches. "Must be a poor family," she said. "Maybe these drawings were however Opa…or whoever…expressed their feelings. Maybe they also used art. Like I do."

She heard a sneeze.

"Yulika?"

Juliana quickly placed the book back in its box and opened the door to the cellar.

"In here." Her cheeks burned with embarrassment at having been caught snooping.

Opa furrowed his brows. "Why would someone young be with old books?"

Juliana shrugged. "I didn't know where else to go. I'm sorry. I'll put everything back."

"That's okay. They're old." Juliana hoped he was being honest and not just polite.

Opa beckoned to her to follow him, and once they were in his bedroom, he invited her to sit on his bed.

"I don't know, Opa. I'm really dirty."

Opa chuckled. "With everything I have been through in my life, a little dust is nothing. Sit down."

Juliana did as she was told.

He patted her shoulder. "I know you've come here because of me. I'm very happy to see you and to spend time with you, Yulika. But I'm very sad that you have changed your life because of my roof damage."

"Roof...?" Juliana was confused.

Opa tapped his head with his finger.

He meant his dementia. And he obviously had a sense of humour about it. Juliana smiled.

"I'm also very happy that my whole family is together for Christmas for the very first time. But it makes me sad that you are not happy."

Now Juliana felt guilty for making Opa unhappy. That

was never her intent. Her anger was always with her parents. Why did it feel like she could never win?

"I didn't want to make you sad, Opa. I'm sorry."

Opa's eyes widened. "Oh! I don't want to make you sadder, Yulika! What I want to say is that I didn't think you might feel…*wie sagt man*…?"

Juliana didn't understand German, which is what she assumed her grandfather just spoke in.

"Your mom, aunt, and uncle are used to it when I speak German sometimes. What word means when things are too much?"

"Overwhelmed?"

Opa nodded. "*Ja.*"

Juliana assumed that meant *yes*.

"I'm used to the big family. The more, the merry."

Juliana smiled. "The merrier."

Opa smiled back at her. "The merrier. Right. I hope Peter and Brian get married and have children someday. Then my family will be bigger."

"That would be cool."

"But they must do it soon, so I'll remember." He pointed to his head. "Roof damage."

Opa was being so kind to Juliana despite her outburst upstairs. That she was only getting to know him now saddened her more.

Opa took in a deep breath. "I love the smell of Christmas. Don't you?"

"It does smell nice upstairs."

Opa laughed heartily. "Yes. Down here…it is not so nice." He patted her on the shoulder again. "Will you join us, Yulika? I already talked to your mom. She will not speak to you like that again in front of everyone. But remember: she is also going through a hard time." He pointed to his head, and the expression on his face darkened. "This is not fun."

Juliana's heart broke as she realized the entire situation wasn't fair for anyone: not for her, not for her parents, and definitely not for her grandfather, who somehow still managed to have fun.

It was almost as though Miss Kasia was giving him advice, too.

"And on Boxing Day," he said, "I will give you some money, and you can go buy yourself something nice.

"Oh, that's okay, Opa. You don't have to."

"I want to. For once, I will get to see what you buy yourself when I give you money." He smiled. He really was looking forward to that.

Juliana missed everything about Calgary. *Everything.* But what was she going to do? Walk home? For better or for worse, Juliana was stuck here, sort of like when they got to a competition with a super slippery stage that was far too small. They just made the best of it. No, it wasn't fair, and she didn't get to go home at the end of the day. But if her grandfather was determined to make her feel welcome—to be her cheerleader—then maybe she should accept his offer.

"Just let me clean myself up."

Opa rubbed her shoulder. "Young people don't like kisses from adults." He really got it, didn't he? "I'll tell them that you're coming."

He showed her the bathroom and where the washcloths were before heading upstairs himself.

The bathroom walls were devoid of the peeling wallpaper and instead painted white. Cracked and sometimes mouldy beige tiles decorated the area around the sink. The shower stall was made of white metal, and in front of it and opposite the sink, where Juliana stood, were the water heater and furnace.

She wiped away at the dust on her dress, but to her dismay the water left marks on the nylon fabric, and she couldn't find a hair dryer. Made sense—Opa was almost bald—but given all the other old things Juliana had found, she'd figured searching for one had been worth a try.

Juliana removed her bobby pins and opted for a quick French braid across the back of her head, wrapping the tail of the braid back on itself, and sticking the pins back in.

"Just have fun, right?" she said to herself in the mirror.

She took a deep breath and went upstairs.

CHAPTER SIXTEEN

"How can Pastor Fröhlich keep ranting on like that about leaving Hungary?" Peter-Bátschi slammed his fist on the table.

"Don't tell me you're happy about it?" Krehling-Bátschi, Susi-Néni's husband, said. Krehling-Bátschi's first name was Adam, so, to avoid confusion with Mammi's deceased brother Adam, all his nieces and nephews called him by his last name.

"Of course not. But it's been done. Let's move on!"

Elisabeth, working in the kitchen, could hear the men as they slammed their fists on the table in the front room, drinking schnapps and conversing about the pastor's Christmas morning sermon. She enjoyed listening in on their conversations; they were much livelier and about bigger things in this world than what the women gossiped about. But one voice was missing in all the discussion: Tata's. He was always one to "move on," as Peter-Bátschi was arguing, and for the same reasons, even if moving on saddened him.

"But what about our children? They're having difficulties with Romanian, and many parents can't help them," Krehling-Bátschi said.

"That's my point!" Peter-Bátschi said. "Instead of going on and on like that and getting everyone angry about the changes, he could be focusing on helping our church's two schools adjust."

As much as Elisabeth wanted to agree with both her father and her uncle, she also felt the fear that Krehling-Bátschi was talking about. What changes would happen in their town? They had wanted to celebrate the one hundredth anniversary of their ancestors' arrival in Semlak this year from the Hungarian town of Mezöberény, but the war and the destruction of the Austro-Hungarian Empire had left everyone feeling less than festive. Did the people in power know their decisions affected everyday people like the Schuhmachers and the Brauns?

"But that he even dared speak about it this morning! We're celebrating the birth of our saviour and he's going on about Hungary!" Peter-Bátschi said again.

Krehling-Bátschi shook his head. "When Lukas returns, everything will be different for him. Poor man. He'll take it all in stride of course, but the Semlak he loves will no longer be a Hungarian village."

The mention of her father caught Elisabeth off guard.

"I don't understand," Luki piped up. "I'm right here."

The men all roared with laughter while Elisabeth swallowed a sob and continued on with her work. While the men enjoyed their drinks in the front room, she, her sisters, Mammi, and several female cousins were hustling about in the kitchen finishing preparations for a full Christmas dinner for lunchtime, with only a work apron protecting their Sunday clothes.

At sixty-one, Omama allowed herself to sit at the kitchen table as she peeled potatoes over the slop pail: she had broken an ankle a year before and could no longer stand for any long period of time.

Her many underskirts bubbled up on her lap as her black pleated outer skirt, protected by a dark-blue apron, tried to contain them all. Her *tschurak* was a little faded after washing it for so many years and hanging it outside to dry. Her black, stiffened kerchief enclosed her face like a triangle, the ties sticking out sideways under her chin. The expression on her face looked as stiff as her kerchief.

"Your mother tells me you're taking over the household," Omama said to Elisabeth, who was slicing a fresh loaf of bread. "It's about time." Potato peels dropped into the pail, splashing into the dirty water that sat above the morning's breakfast waste. All of it would be carried out later and fed to the pigs.

Elisabeth tried not to frown as she carried a loaf of

bread past Omama and set it on the dining table. When she returned, Omama continued.

"You're old enough to take on that work. Martin Luther taught us that work will bring us closer to God."

Elisabeth knew what was coming next. She forced a smile as she sliced another loaf.

"And all that reading you do is not bringing you closer to God," Omama said.

"I read the Bible and Martin Luther's teachings, Omama." Elisabeth then quoted from what she'd read last night: "Luther says, 'Until the heart believes in God, it is impossible for it to rejoice in Him. When faith is lacking, man is filled with fear and gloom and is disposed to flee at the very mention, the mere thought, of God.'"

"And God judges favourably those who study His words. But if it were up to me, I would have your father's books burned: they will only tempt you to ignore your responsibilities."

Elisabeth shuddered at the comment. Mammi took some of the peeled potatoes and began cutting them up. "She'll no longer have time, Modr. There's much too much work to do around here." Omama gave an affirming nod.

Using some dish towels to protect her hand, Elisabeth opened the iron door to the oven and checked the goose she had butchered the other day. The skin was browning up nicely, and the rich aroma from the dripping fat made Elisabeth's stomach growl. She closed the oven door.

"I think the goose will be done within the hour," Elisabeth announced, hoping to change the subject.

"Then help Omama with the potatoes," Mammi directed, wiping her hands on her apron. "Anna, take a pot outside and fill it with water."

"Do I have to?" Anna complained. "It's bitterly cold!" Mammi raised a hand to indicate she was about to hit her daughter, and Anna dropped her chin, apologized quietly, switched her house shoes for boots, and asked Elisabeth to pass her a cooking pot.

"Do you want to use my new mittens?" Rosina offered. She had been allowed to open her gift that morning—also a new pair of mittens Mammi had knit.

But one look at Mammi and Anna obviously resigned herself to no mittens as her punishment. She slipped on her boots and left.

"Lissa," Omama said to Mammi, "you should have slapped her. That's no way to raise a child."

Mammi sighed. "I know, Modr, but I'm far too busy right now to deal with her tears."

"Then you insist she not cry. They'll never learn without discipline."

Mammi carried the second loaf of sliced bread to the back room, got a damp cloth, and wiped up the bread crumbs on the kitchen table. She then took the cutting board over to the washing table.

Elisabeth was dying to ask if she could open her gift from last night, but she tried to heed Luther's words, to rejoice only in God and not in silver or gold.

Or presents wrapped in brown paper.

A hand banged on the table in the front room, which the men often did when making a point.

"Why lament about Empress Sisi? She died—when was it? Over twenty years ago now," Peter-Bátschi said.

"Empress Sisi?" Omama's face softened and she raised her voice to join in the conversation from her spot in the kitchen. "She was practically as old as I am now when that horrid Italian man stabbed her."

Peter-Bátschi, who was sitting with his back to the kitchen, turned around. "And you're just as lovely as she was, Modr."

Omama flapped her hand at him and smiled, her face turning into a raisin. "Now you're being dishonest."

Elisabeth had finished peeling three potatoes with her knife and was about to start on the fourth one when she couldn't hold it in anymore: she had to ask. As the conversation about the late empress of the former Austro-Hungarian Empire continued through the kitchen, she crept over to her mother. Part of her was screaming inside, telling her to stop and continue with her duties, but a bigger, stronger part was pulling her toward Mammi.

Elisabeth spoke in a low voice. "I'm really sorry about last night. I was just so excited about my gift. I saw what the others had got but noticed that mine had a different shape and weight. I just couldn't wait to open it."

Mammi's eyes flashed with anger at Elisabeth. "Is that still on your mind?"

Elisabeth shrank into her blouse and *tschurak*.

"Do you really believe God wants you to focus on gifts instead of your family and your behaviour?"

Elisabeth shook her head.

"Good. If you mention it one more time, you can pull out the box of corn kernels yourself."

Elisabeth bit her lip to stop it from quivering. She wanted to run to her bed and hide under her blanket, but so long as the men were in the front room, she had nowhere to run.

She wiped her tears with the back of her hand, returned to the kitchen table, and kept peeling. If Omama had noticed anything, she didn't say.

THE MEN WERE ONCE AGAIN in the front room, now divided into groups of three and playing cards and drinking more schnapps and getting even louder. Luki was sitting beside Krehling-Bátschi, who was teaching him how to play. The women were in the kitchen, cleaning up.

Stacks upon stacks of dishes sat piled on the table next to three washing bowls, and three of Elisabeth's cousins had lined up, each one in charge of one bowl: one for the first rinse, one to wash and scrub, and a third for a final rinse. Mammi and Rosina stood at the end of the line to dry the dishes and put them away.

Elisabeth was in charge of making a light soup for supper, so she started the broth that would simmer on the stove the rest of the day. She stood at the kitchen table and snapped the bones from the goose apart. Anna helped her.

"You asked me about Tata," Anna whispered. Elisabeth stopped breaking the bones and listened. "I couldn't hear him sing at Christmas service this morning." Anna sniffled. "He always sings so loud."

"Elisabeth," Omama called over, "idle hands are the work of the devil."

Elisabeth continued pulling the goose apart, but slowly, so she could hear her sister's quiet voice.

"And he didn't cut the goose this year," Anna went on. "Krehling-Bátschi did it."

Elisabeth understood what her sister meant, and she also knew that everyone else had noticed it. The silence as everyone looked around the table to see who would cut the goose had filled their home. Normally, it would be the next man in the household, but Luki was far too young to use a knife that large. Krehling-Bátschi was the eldest man at the table and so was given the honour.

Elisabeth wiped a hand on her apron and then lay it on Anna's shoulder. Rosina, walking a plate to the kitchen cupboard, stopped by her sisters, and, judging by her red eyes, had also been crying.

"I miss Tata," Rosina whispered, and Elisabeth rubbed her back to show she understood.

"Mammi," Elisabeth said, "may Rosina help us with the soup?"

Rosina placed the clean plate in the proper pile on its shelf and looked at their mother hopefully. Mammi nodded. "We can work faster without you."

"Here," Elisabeth said and pulled out a chair for Rosina to kneel on. She passed her the uneaten potatoes and a paring knife and asked her to cut the potatoes smaller while Elisabeth continued with the goose carcass. Anna squeezed past Omama to retrieve the last of the uneaten food, and came back with a serving bowl of sliced carrots and sauerkraut.

"Throw them in," Elisabeth instructed, and Anna did.

"I'm going to get more water," Elisabeth said. "Keep adding to the pot." She picked up the slop pail on her way to take it out back to the animals. Elisabeth knew the girls needed to get their minds off their father's absence, and so did she. Her gift could wait: Elisabeth needed to help her sisters right now.

"Good. You're making yourself useful," Omama said as she watched from her chair while Elisabeth switched her shoes, and Elisabeth scowled, her face turned away so no one could see.

CHAPTER SEVENTEEN

*J*uliana sat on her sleeping bag in her green circle skirt and simple, cream blouse, having just returned from Christmas morning service at a Lutheran church with her parents and Opa. Now she had an hour or so to wake up: church had been so boring she'd almost fallen asleep if it weren't for the occasional standing and sitting. *At least I got in a few squats,* she thought.

She was flipping through the book of drawings, trying to piece together the life the artist—Opa?—had led, when someone knocked at her door. She quickly—but cautiously—shoved the book under her pillow before her parents entered the room.

"Hey, sweetie," Mom said.

Juliana responded with a weak smile. The next stop

on the Christmas celebration train was Aunt Anne's house so they could celebrate with Uncle Phillip's family. The last thing Juliana wanted right now was to spend more time with all the people she'd humiliated herself in front of last night, and then meet a bunch more she didn't know: Uncle Phillip was one of eight siblings, and he and Aunt Anne had a home that was apparently large enough to hold them all, their families included, though it'd be a bit squished.

Hence the weak smile.

Dad sat down at the edge of her sleeping bag and brought out a large, flat, rectangular package wrapped in cheesy snowmen wrapping paper and topped with a red bow. He lay it on the bed. "Your mom and I had a talk about you last night."

"I know," Juliana said. "I could hear my name through our doors."

Her parents looked surprised as Mom joined them on the floor.

"But I couldn't hear what you were talking about," Juliana admitted. "Listen, about last night." She stared at her hands. "I got…overwhelmed."

She didn't look up, but from the side she could see Dad scratch the back of his neck. He was either about to drop a bomb on her or apologize. One of the two. Hopefully the latter.

"We also wanted to apologize for yesterday evening."

Juliana breathed a sigh of relief.

"Tata mentioned that maybe we'd overdone it. Just because we're your parents doesn't…"

…mean we're perfect.

"…mean we're perfect."

Her parents said that a lot.

But as much as she appreciated that her parents apologized—she knew not everyone's did—she wanted to know what was inside the gift. It looked about one metre by one-and-a-half metres, and maybe three or four centimetres thick.

That was about the size of a tap board.

Or two bulletin boards, if her parents were going to give her something boring.

But a tap board? Were her parents about to give her a tap board? Could she just open it now?

"Are you listening?" Mom asked, and only then did Juliana realize she'd actually been staring at the gift instead of pretending to be paying attention to her parents.

She repeated Mom's last words: "Just because you're my parents doesn't mean you're perfect." Thank god Mom hadn't said anything original.

"Right," Mom confirmed. "And we wanted to give you this."

Dad slid the gift over to Juliana. "We were going to give it to you this evening, but you look like you can't—"

"Paul," Mom interrupted, "just let her open it."

Juliana tore away the wrapping paper.

"Well?" Mom said.

Juliana's jaw dropped. She was right! A wooden tap board with foam cushioning underneath that was big enough to practise on without killing her shins or sliding on carpet.

"We know not being able to dance since we left Calgary has been hard on you," Dad said. "And we don't know if we'll be able to turn the rec room downstairs into any kind of practice studio for you. Aside from the fact that it's not our house, the ceiling is low, the floor underneath the carpet is cement, and we may need to use the room for entertaining."

Juliana nodded. "It was pretty crowded in the kitchen last night."

Mom smiled, but Juliana couldn't tell if it was a genuine smile or the one Mom used when she was about to assign Juliana a chore. "Tomorrow morning, you and I can take a vacuum cleaner and duster to the basement. No need for you to be tapping while you're sneezing your brains out."

The "chore" smile. Juliana had to help clean that disgusting room even though the dust hadn't been her fault? But then again, they were here to help Opa, and his Alzheimer's wasn't his fault either.

"And when we get home this evening," Dad said, "you can connect to mine or your mom's phone and call Rachel on one of your apps."

Juliana let out a sigh of relief. Her parents headed for the door.

"We love you," Mom said.

"Yup!" Normally, Juliana hated mush. But under the circumstances, she would take it.

Her parents nodded, smiled, and left.

THE DAY over and a two-hour phone call with Rachel behind her—part of it while attached via her power cord to the wall, but at least in the privacy of her room—Juliana now wanted to solve the mystery of the journal. She pulled the book back out from under her pillow. Her parents said they were going to watch TV in their bedroom before calling it quits for the day. It was a good time to talk with Opa.

The hallway floor creaked under her feet, a sound she was finally getting used to.

Wonder if I could turn that rhythm into a dance some day? she thought and filed the idea in the back of her mind.

She peeked into the living room, and Opa was sitting there, smiling at the wall.

"Opa?"

He snapped to, took a moment to see who'd called him, and a big grin appeared on his face. "My Yulika," he said. "You look lovely."

Juliana blushed.

"You take after your mother that way. Not so much your father."

Juliana giggled. "Well, Dad does spend most of his time sitting in a truck." She smoothed out her skirt with one hand, holding the book in her other behind her back. "Opa? Can I ask you something?"

"Of course." He patted the spot beside him on the couch.

She sat down and pulled out the book. "Who did this belong to?"

Opa took the book in his hands and opened the cover. He read the writing on the front page and his eyes lit up, his sagging cheeks plumped out, and his smile appeared again. He closed the cover, turned the book over in his hands, opened it again, and leafed through some of the pages.

"Where did you find this?"

Juliana's cheeks burned: she felt like she'd been caught again. "Last night…when I went into the cellar."

"Ah, when you were angry with everyone."

"Well, not everyone. Just Mom and Dad."

"For a child, that is everyone."

He turned over more pages and seemed to be studying the drawings. His fingers came close to touching the pages but he held them back. Was it out of some kind of fear?

"I hope you didn't touch the pages," he said.

Juliana's neck disappeared as her head shrunk into her shoulders. "I was really careful…"

He patted her on the knee. "It's all right. But please

don't ever again. These are pencil drawings, and the oils in your fingers will smear them."

Juliana nodded fervently. "Who made them?"

But Opa didn't seem to hear her question. He opened the book to the front again and stopped at the first drawing.

"That's the kitchen she grew up in," he said.

"Who?"

He pointed to the cube with the dark door on the left of the drawing. "Over here is the stove and *backofa*."

"And what?"

"*Backofa*."

He'd heard her, so she asked her first question again. "Who did the drawings?"

"And look at that…she even included part of the kitchen table and chairs."

"Opa, who?"

"They used to heat that *backofa* with cornstalks. See? They're in the basket."

Juliana was beginning to lose her patience. Why wasn't he listening to her?

He looked at the drawing some more, then chuckled to himself. "I remember her telling me about that Christmas: it was the first one after Opa had left for America. She had tried so hard to please Oma. Oma was often angry, and strict, but she was even angrier then. She didn't even let her open her Christmas gift on Christmas Eve. It was only many years later that Mammi realized it was Oma's way of just getting through that Christmas."

His opa? His oma? His mommy? Juliana thought for a moment. So, this drawing, and all the rest in the book were made by…his mother.

"My great-grandmother Elisabeth," she said, but Opa didn't react.

"Look at that. No phone back then." Then his face changed, as though he was suddenly remembering something else.

"I have to call Karl. I have to wish him Merry Christmas."

Karl? Juliana didn't recognize the name.

Opa set the book on the coffee table and headed for the phone.

Juliana picked up the book and studied that first drawing again. Her great-grandmother Elisabeth, the ancestor Juliana had been named after. These were her drawings, depictions of her life.

This book was her art.

But Mom had never talked about her, just like Mom almost never talked about her background in general.

Why?

Juliana glanced out the doorway and into the kitchen, where Opa was dialling. This house had just one phone, attached to the wall. That meant her mom and siblings had had to share that one phone in the kitchen. Juliana and her parents each had their own phone.

"Karl?" Opa said, and then began to speak in German. He laughed, then a minute later turned serious only to laugh again. He listened and then banged his fist against the wall. She had no idea what he was saying, but he seemed happy.

No phone when this drawing had been created. Juliana had learned about early Canadian settlers. She had also learned about ancient civilizations and all that. But it had never really occurred to her what life might have been like without a phone.

I would've had to write letters to Rachel and probably wait for weeks or even months for a response, she thought. Suddenly, not having been able to talk to her best friend for a few hours, or at most a day, didn't seem so bad.

She headed back to her room, checked the time on her phone, and figured hitting the sack a little early wouldn't be a bad thing. Opa obviously remembered the book, so she'd just have to ask him more about it another day.

CHAPTER EIGHTEEN

"Can't we get undressed?" Elisabeth asked. After all the food from the afternoon, her multiple underskirts were beginning to hurt against her stomach. She wasn't sure if she'd have space for the soup she and her sisters had made.

"The day is not over yet," Mammi admonished. "We may still get visitors."

The sun was already at the horizon. It was late in the afternoon, and all Elisabeth could think of was sleep and comfortable clothes. Unable to change the situation, though, she headed to the front room, where it was nice and warm, and pulled down an encyclopedia. The house was clean, her sisters were joyfully playing with the dolls they'd received from Mammi's family, and Luki was occupied with the rubber ball and jacks that had been his gift.

Elisabeth had received a lovely white handkerchief to be used at her confirmation. From Tata's family, they had received plentiful food.

Mammi occupied herself in the back room, reading the Bible while knitting a sock.

Elisabeth lit a few gas lamps, placed them on the table, and then opened up the encyclopedia to an entry on international transportation. Across the top it said,

ÜBERSICHTSKARTE DES WELTVERKEHRS.

The map showed the routes that ships took to travel through the oceans and those that trains took to carry passengers through countries. Although the set had been published thirty years before, Elisabeth guessed that these routes hadn't changed: she couldn't imagine railways laying tracks and then ripping them up again or shipping companies changing routes that already looked quite direct. There might be more transportation now, especially with the war over and life returning back to normal, but certainly not less.

Tata had been gone for almost a month now. She traced a rail line with her finger, passing through empires that no longer existed: the Holy German Empire and the Austro-Hungarian Empire. Then she followed the shipping line from Bremen to New York. She didn't know how he had arrived in Pennsylvania, though: the map was too small to show her those rail lines.

"Elisabeth!" Rosina came running in, her face all aglow. "Maria and her family are coming!"

Elisabeth's heart immediately lit up as she glanced out a window to see the Haibachs walking toward the house. Finally, someone she could actually talk to about Tata!

The girls waved to each other through the window.

Before Elisabeth could close the book to put it back, Rosina came over for a peek.

"What are you reading?"

Elisabeth showed where they were and then where Tata hopefully was, in Pennsylvania, America.

"That's not too far," Rosina said, and Elisabeth knew better than to correct her youngest sibling about this. Better that she should believe that Tata was close.

"Elisabeth!" Luki called. "Maria's here!"

"I know, Luki!" Elisabeth laughed, delighted at the unannounced visit. "I'm coming!" She closed the encyclopedia, placed it back up on the shelf, and headed into the kitchen. Mammi carried the guests' winter attire into the back room, and the parents, Haibach Adam and Haibach Anna, greeted Elisabeth quickly and then followed Mammi inside to the formally decorated back room. Maria's brother, Joschka, and Luki climbed under the kitchen table and played with Luki's rubber ball and jacks. Rosina and Anna stole away to the table in the front room.

"Merry Christmas!" Maria said as she hugged Elisabeth. Elisabeth embraced her best friend: seeing her now in their home was the blessing Elisabeth sorely needed.

Maria had somehow survived falling through the ice on the Marosch River, being hit by a bicycle when she ran across the street to greet Elisabeth, and lighting the tips of her hair when she had had her back turned to the stove. She may have been a year older, but definitely not a year wiser. However, if Elisabeth ever needed to talk to someone, Maria was the one who would listen. Now, Elisabeth sniffled as all the feelings she'd tried so hard to suppress began pouring out and into her embrace.

Maria gently pushed Elisabeth back and Elisabeth wiped her eyes.

"What's wrong?" Maria offered Elisabeth her handkerchief.

Elisabeth shook her head as though to say, "Nothing," but Maria obviously knew better.

"Are you missing your father at Christmas?"

Elisabeth nodded as she dabbed her eyes, and Maria led her to the large sofa in the front room. They sat down, and Maria took Elisabeth's hand in hers.

"Tell me about it," she said, and Elisabeth began to cry, though she tried to stay quiet so her sisters under the table wouldn't hear as they continued playing with their dolls.

"I can't stop missing him," Elisabeth said. "I'm trying so hard to take care of my chores, but I can't seem to control my feelings the way Mammi wants me to."

Rosina and Anna peeked out from under the table and eventually crawled out. Anna, usually nervous around too much emotion, stayed back, but Rosina gave Elisabeth a hug.

Everything Elisabeth had experienced came out: Tata's voice missing from Christmas service, Krehling-Bátschi serving the goose, Elisabeth now having to take over the household so Mammi could make shoes. The only thing she left out was her gift: she didn't want Mammi to hear her complain about still not having opened it.

Then Mammi did actually call Elisabeth.

"Yes?" Elisabeth dried her eyes and blew her nose.

"Bring us some cookies and tea!"

"Yes, Mammi." She looked at the three girls surrounding her. "Thank you." Their sad eyes gave her little comfort, though; she knew she had just shown her sisters that she wasn't strong enough to deal with Tata being away. She glanced up at the crucifix above the door. How often had she prayed to Him only to receive silence as her answer?

You wouldn't understand, anyway. Josef was on earth, always with You.

Elisabeth grabbed a pot, tied on her boots, and headed outside to fetch water. She grasped the handle on the well and turned it as fast as she could, lowering the bucket deep into the ground.

You could turn water into wine and feed thousands. What do You know of my existence? she asked Jesus. *What can You possibly understand of it?*

The bucket hit the water and she reversed her movements, pulling the now heavy bucket back up. *All the miracles You performed and I can't even get a pot of water to boil fast. But You did it all in the name of—*

The answer came to her. Was it Jesus talking to her? Or was it her own thoughts? She couldn't tell. But she had an answer.

Josef was Your father here on earth, because Your real father lived in Heaven. You never saw Your real father, but You knew Him. In Your heart, You knew Him.

Despite the cold weather, a warm feeling grew within Elisabeth. Tata would be gone for about a year. In that time, though, he was alive in her heart. She could pray for his safety and well-being, and once he mailed them back his address, she would write him every week. It wasn't going to be easy, and it wasn't the same as having him home, but this knowledge would—she hoped—get her and her siblings through this.

Elisabeth carried the pot back inside.

BACK IN THE front room with Maria, her mood much uplifted, Elisabeth nibbled on another cookie and sipped on some chamomile tea.

"Your mother's cookies are astounding," Maria said after she finished her sixth one.

"Actually, I made these."

Maria's eyebrows jumped up. "Only fourteen and you

can bake like this already? The decorations you made with the icing are exquisite. You'll make your husband very happy!"

Elisabeth's cheeks warmed and she nodded. "Mammi taught me last year, showed me again this year, and then left me on my own to do it while she packed Tata's belongings. You have to make sure the butter stays cold in your hands, so I opened the window in the kitchen and pushed the table over to it."

Both girls giggled.

"Didn't it get cold in the house?" Maria asked.

"I closed both doors to the other rooms and just worked fast. Even Tata was impressed. Last year, it took me four hours to get batches ready for the oven, and this year I did it in maybe an hour."

Elisabeth could now say "Tata" without wanting to cry. She knew where he really was, and for now at least, she could accept it.

"But I had to scrub the floor that much harder on the weekend—pushing the table had created grooves all along it."

"Next time just get your brother to help you carry it."

"I think Luki would actually push down and make deeper grooves for me to clean."

Rosina and Anna nodded in agreement.

"We'll help instead," Anna added.

Mammi appeared in the doorway, holding Elisabeth's

gift out to her. Her usually stern face looked surprisingly at ease.

"Jesus would approve of your behaviour today, Lissika. I trust you've learned your lesson?"

Elisabeth nodded. Ignoring her racing heart, she slowly stood up, approached her mother, and extended her hand. Mammi placed the gift in it and waited while Elisabeth untied the twine and carefully unwrapped the brown-paper-wrapped package. She gasped.

In her hands she held a blank leather-bound drawing book, three pencils of different thicknesses, and a thick pad of paper.

"Patience is a virtue," Mammi said. "Never forget that. In fact, your father bought this months ago, when he last travelled to Arad, knowing you would soon be running out of paper in your old book. He also knew you would want to write him while he was away. He wanted to give you the gift as soon as he returned, but I told him to wait until Christmas."

Elisabeth's smile stretched from ear to ear, and tears of happiness welled in her eyes.

"I regret you won't have much time to use the book," Mammi said. "Housework is much more important. It's a shame God gave you such a useless gift, but he gave it to you nonetheless. You will need to use it from time to time to honour Him."

So much happiness flowed through Elisabeth that she ignored Mammi's hurtful words.

"Now I must get back to our guests," Mammi said and returned to the back room, her black skirt brushing against the doorway.

"Elisabeth, it's beautiful," Maria said. "What are you going to draw first?"

Elisabeth opened the front cover and saw a note from Tata.

My Golden One,

You have a gift from God, and you must use it. I regret that I will not be able to see your drawings while I am gone, but I do expect to see them when I return. Keep them safe. I do not know what plans God has for your gift, but you have a duty to use it.

Take care of our family, and write me often.

Tata

"Well?" Maria asked just as a rubber ball rolled into the room.

"Maybe I'll start with the most important room in the house," Elisabeth said as she picked up the ball and shot Luki a look.

"Which is?"

Elisabeth walked into the kitchen, rolled the ball under the table to the two boys, and then leaned against the washing table.

"What are you doing?" Luki asked, peering out from under the table.

"Drawing," Elisabeth replied. She changed her angle slightly so she wouldn't get Maria's brother and Luki in the picture.

"Why here?" Maria asked.

"We spend time in all the rooms in the house, but this is where we cook," Elisabeth replied. "Just as Jesus fed thousands with bread and fish, we fed dozens today with bread, one bird, and some vegetables. Because we don't go hungry, our family exists. Hopefully it will for generations."

Elisabeth began sketching the crucifix above the doorway.

CHAPTER NINETEEN

It was Boxing Day. Juliana helped Mom clean the rec room that morning, and when they'd finished, she was ecstatic to see the retro décor in all its glory, from the popcorn ceiling to the—vacuumed—shag carpet and peeling cream wallpaper. Even the furniture, in its fabrics of browns, oranges, and puke greens (what else could she call it?) practically sparkled. She couldn't wait to show Sophie, who'd be dropping by later in the afternoon to hang out again. Juliana would use the gift money from Opa to treat Sophie: not only would that make Sophie happy, but also Opa, because if there was one thing Juliana had learned since arriving in Kitchener a few days ago, it was that family made Opa happy.

Despite her anger toward her parents for not including her in any of these discussions, Juliana had to admit that this new family had made her laugh a few times. She was still angry with her parents for treating her like a little kid, but the more she thought about what Opa had tried to tell her — that this situation wasn't fair to anyone — the easier it became to focus on having fun.

Now, with Dad cleaning up the garage for the moving truck tomorrow, and Mom with Opa at Opa's old friend Karl's house, Juliana could finally enjoy some time to herself.

Down in the basement, standing on the tap board, her tap shoes already on, she stood in complete silence. No parents to please, no strange family to make conversation with, just her new tap board, her shoes, and whatever rhythm she wanted to start with. Music was not an option today, not so much because she only had the poor speakers on her smartphone, but because she didn't want *anything* telling her what to do, not even music.

She wanted to decide what to do.

She outlined the tap board with her feet, her taps scraping along its surface.

Looks like a piece of paper, she thought. She took a moment to remember the drawing of the kitchen and then began reproducing it with her feet, scraping her taps along the board in long lines and short lines, squiggling and shimmying her feet where her great-grandmother had filled in some shading. The partial chairs and table, the doorway, the window behind it, the cross above it, and then the oven.

What did Opa call it? She thought for a moment and the word came to her. *Backofa.* Even though the white cube with the small dark door didn't look anything like an oven to Juliana, she figured maybe back then—whenever that was—they didn't have regular ovens.

"*BACKofa.*" Emphasis on the first syllable. ONE and two.

Juliana created a basic combo to the rhythm of the word.

BACKofa—ONE and two, *BACKofa*—THREE and four.

BACKofa—*STOMP* heel *stamp*, *BACKofa*—*STOMP* heel heel.

And so Juliana continued, the simple rhythm relaxing her muscles—from her feet all the way through her legs, torso, arms, and up to her head—as her body sank into the repetitive steps.

She'd wanted to ask Opa more questions today, but he seemed a little out of sorts. Even Mom and Dad had noticed it, so Juliana had left the book under her pillow.

BACKofa—*STOMP* heel *stamp*, *BACKofa*—*STOMP* heel heel.

But, also that morning, Mom had gotten a phone call from Juliana's new studio, Kitchener Dance Academy. The school offered more than just dance, despite its name, and was easily four times the size of Juliana's old studio back home. Judging by videos from last year, her new dance team alone had almost thirty members, massive compared to her old team of ten.

BACKofa—STOMP heel stamp, BACKofa—STOMP heel heel.

To say that the sheer size of the new team made Juliana nervous was an understatement. But when she had looked up the studio online back home, she saw that they offered everything: singing, drama, guitar, tap, jazz, ballet, contemporary, acro…the works!

Juliana switched up her little combo.

ONE and two, THREE and four became and ONE and two and three and four.

Heel STOMP ball change, flap ball change.

But Mom had registered her only for dance, worried that Juliana would get overwhelmed if she took on too much. Even pulling out all her report cards to show Mom the steady stream of As, Excellents, and Well Dones she had earned couldn't sway her.

"You have to write your exams in January, and you're going to be busy meeting new friends and wanting to join half the extracurricular groups at school. I know you, Juliana," she'd said.

And Dad had agreed.

"Once your mom and I start working, we're not going to be here all the time to help you with your responsibilities."

Juliana began a series of running flaps, though she had

nowhere to go. The peeling wallpaper blurred in her vision as the sounds from her feet filled her ears. Her heart racing, her body sweating, her feet moving faster and faster.

But when had her parents last helped her with her homework? She loved learning: science excited her as much as English and French, math as much as history and geography. She was always on top of her work, always striving for the best marks. What gave them the right to tell her what she could and couldn't do?

Juliana's muscles started to hurt, but she kept pushing as her body shunted its energy to her feet, and the flaps gave way to a barrage of triple taps, pull-backs, cramp rolls, shuffles, flams...whatever she felt like doing. For once, Juliana was in control.

And only through dance could she begin to express what was storming through her with this upheaval she'd just endured. The loneliness, the shock, the confusion, the embarrassment.

But also the discovery: What was her great-grandmother like, and what stories had she captured in that book?

Her feet started to slow down, her body tiring from the exertion. After a few more minutes, she dropped to the floor.

Well, the tap board. Sitting all sweaty on the shag rug just somehow felt gross.

Juliana opened the book, which she'd hidden under a sweater in case anyone came down unexpectedly, and studied the first two drawings again. They looked like they'd been drawn by someone who loved to draw…but not by someone who'd been doing it for decades.

"Opa had said this was the kitchen his mother had grown up in. So…this is the kitchen of her childhood. And her father had left for the States some year and she had tried really hard to impress her mother, but she did something wrong and didn't get her Christmas gift right away. No one does that to an adult. That's how you punish children," she said aloud. "So…my great-grandmother must have drawn these when she was young. But young like my cousin Scott? Or young like me?"

She studied the drawings again. They were too good for an eight-year-old and looked closer to the sketches of the more talented students in Juliana's art class—maybe the year below—from back in junior high. If Juliana's great-grandmother Elisabeth had drawn these sketches when she was about Juliana's age, then this journal contained the story of a teenage girl from a very long time ago.

Juliana wasn't happy with the move. In fact, she still hated it and would rather be in Calgary. But that didn't mean that holding another teenager's story—another teenager's art!—from so long ago in her hands wasn't very special. It had already influenced Juliana's art, had already helped her heal just a little.

What more about the girl in the diary could Juliana learn?

SETTING THE RECORD
STRAIGHT

Between Worlds is a work of fiction that tells both a contemporary and historical story. In both parts of the book, I've included facts about life during the time period in which the story is set. In writing novels, the story always comes first (because otherwise this would be a history textbook), so this section explains any important facts that may have been changed and adds more background to the story. If you have any questions about what you've read in this, or in any of the other books in the series, ask away! Email me at author@loriwolfheffner.com.

SEMLAK, ROMANIA

Semlak (now spelled Semlac) is indeed a village in Romania, though very few Germans live there anymore. It's in

Arad County, in a valley along the Marosch River (Mureș in Romanian), and is four kilometres long from end to end. Arad, the central city of the county, is about thirty-seven kilometres away, and Temeswar (Timișoara), in neighbouring Timiș County, is about ninety kilometres away. Although not "in the middle of nowhere" for North Americans, it certainly was for the people of the day: the nearest train station was three kilometres away but across the river, and so it could only be reached by cable ferry. Today, Semlak has its own train station.

Thanks to the online genealogy group Donauschwaben Villages Helping Hands, and to the German non-profit Heimatortsgemeinschaft Semlak, I was able to reconstruct much of the living situation in Semlak at the time, although I also had to invent various details.

For example, the typical farmer's house did have only three rooms, and the family did sleep all in the same one. (You can visit www.dvhh.org and www.semlak.de for more information.)

However, I don't know for sure what books a family like Elisabeth's would have had, if any at all. Day-to-day living, and conforming to the community's unspoken rules, dictated everyday behaviour. The Lutheran church congregation supported two to three schools, depending on finances, and these schools only went to grade six. Grade seven was necessary to attend secondary school, so if anyone did seek further education, they would have had to travel out of the village. (It would be another several years before grade seven was introduced to these church-funded schools, despite a postwar Romanian law requiring that it happen sooner.)

The story about the bells is true: as World War I progressed, church bells were taken down and melted to make cannons. However, I don't know if the German villagers would have used other bells on an occasion as special as Christmas to replace such a beautiful sound. A new large bell for the village's Lutheran church was purchased in 1920.

THE SCHUHMACHERS

A great-grandfather of mine, Mathias Heffner, was a shoemaker who lived in a Danube Swabian town in Hungary, so I took inspiration from him for Tata's trade and for the family's name.

Elisabeth is inspired by—but is *not*—my great-grandmother Katharina Wolf. My Omama Wolf was born in Semlak, attended the Lutheran church, and cherished her family, but she also had a sharp tongue, meaning she wasn't the gentle, innocent "village girl" one often romanticizes in historical fiction. However, in postcards she wrote to her granddaughters in Canada years later, you can hear her sadness; the Iron Curtain the Communist dictatorships had drawn prevented her from ever seeing her son after World War II, or his children in Canada. Some postcards were indeed meant for her granddaughters once they were old enough, but their messages were delivered decades after her passing. My mother told me that they had actually completed all the paperwork for Omama Wolf to immigrate, but she died before she could travel.

But what Katharina Wolf thought about the changes that affected her village and way of life, I'll never know. That's where Katharina Wolf ends and Elisabeth Schuhmacher begins. I had to free myself from the pressure of trying to accurately represent an ancestor whose memory still lived in others, even if only faintly.

You may have noticed that Elisabeth does a lot of housework, and that she hopes to marry one day. This was normal for her time and culture. World War I had just begun to shake things up, but there was still a strong desire to maintain the community's way of life as it had existed for generations.

You may have also noticed that the parents used corporal punishment to discipline their children. This was, unfortunately, commonplace, and erasing it from the story doesn't erase it from history. My grandfather, John Heffner Sr., Mathias Heffner's son, was fourteen years younger than Elisabeth and came from a different town. He wrote in his memoir that, if he had gotten into any mischief on his way home from school, the telephone-free communication system worked so efficiently that his mother was often already standing at the door with the stick when he walked in.

Naming conventions in Semlak and other German

villages in Eastern Europe differed from ours. For example, it was normal to refer to people by their last name first: Meier Josef or Haibach Anna. This helped villagers differentiate between all those with the same first name. As reported in the book *Semlak*, for example, from 1819-2000, the top ten girls' names accounted for 87% of all 4,092 girls' names in the village, and the top ten boys' names for 82% of all 4,205 boys' names. Nicknames abounded to help separate people. These could have been based on someone's occupation or a noticeable (usually unflattering) characteristic of some kind, or they could have been a short form of the person's name.

One naming convention I strayed from was addressing acquaintances and friends. I believe that writing about this culture in English means losing some of the context that would have signalled to a person living in that village, and at that time, what form of address to use. For example, the added words *Bátschi* for *uncle* and *Néni* for *aunt* were used not only for actual relatives but also for anyone who was at least half a generation older than the speaker. You, a reader of this book, are at a disadvantage, because you obviously don't know the entire congregation and you can't see each character to judge their age unless I break from the story to give you a description. I don't know about you, but I would find that tedious very quickly! A third factor is linguistic: just as French and Spanish have multiple pronouns you can use when addressing someone directly, so does German. Having multiple forms of address would also have helped the inhabitants of Semlak, and of other villages like it, to keep everyone straight. However, English has simplified to only one form: *you*. Therefore, I stayed with the more standard German *Herr* for *Mr.* and *Frau* for *Mrs.*, even though historically in these towns these forms of address were reserved for educated professionals: clergymen, doctors, teachers, etc.

The repetition of first names within a family is historically accurate. To me, this shows just how important the family, both nuclear and extended, was in the lives of Danube Swabians. For example, one ancestor of mine gave birth to fourteen or sixteen children. (The church records differ from family accounts.) Of those, only four grew up to become adults, and of the children who had died in childhood, four were girls called Elisabeth, named after this same ancestor. It's in her honour, and in theirs, that I named Elisabeth in this series.

OTHER SEMLAKERS

The only real person in the novel is Pastor Fröhlich, who, I have read, was very much against Semlak's transfer to Romania and strongly supported Semlak's connection to Hungary—to its culture, and its language. He was apparently responsible for several controversies within the church and the schools it funded, and I can't wait to explore them further.

It was common for Germans in Eastern Europe to

travel to the US to earn money, and in the case of the villagers of Semlak, Pennsylvania seemed to be a preferred destination. I believe an ancestor of mine made the trip twice, though he returned and lived out the rest of his life in his home village, his *heimat*.

MARTIN LUTHER IN ENGLISH

I had a difficult time selecting how best to represent Luther's original teachings, because in the research I had conducted, there were no contemporary (or close to contemporary) English translations of his work, and as it was, English back then differed considerably from our English today. (Think of it this way: Martin Luther died eighteen years before Shakespeare was born.) So, for the English translations of Luther's sermons, I referred to the links published at sermons.martinluther.us.

THE ROTHS AND KITCHENER, ONTARIO

All characters in the present-day timeline are fictional, though the city of Kitchener is very real. (And I don't think of it as a dipstick city!) Kitchener does have a sizeable German population, but the younger generations rarely speak German anymore.

If you're interested in learning more about German culture in Kitchener, visit www.lib.uwaterloo.ca and search for "Lori Heffner" to find my thesis. It's called "Heritage

Languages: The Case of German in Kitchener-Waterloo." I interviewed three generations of three families of German heritage and discussed how German was or wasn't passed on through the generations. Warning: it makes for dry reading and not the best writing, but it shows how the German language gradually disappeared in the three families I interviewed. On the upside, all interview transcripts are included. It's free to download.

Or head over to Amazon to purchase *The Germans of Waterloo Region*, published in 2022, edited by Mathias Schulze, Grit Liebscher, and Sebastian Siebel-Achenbach. It's a culmination of over one hundred oral history interviews. I wrote one chapter in it (under Lori Straus, my married name) and helped coordinate the project.

STAY IN TOUCH!

If you enjoyed the book, sign up for my monthly newsletter! I write it myself, so it's my words to you. You'll get the following:

- Sneak peeks at upcoming books
- Updates about online and in-person appearances
- Book and writing recommendations
- Recipes I love
- Contests
- And more!

Visit BetweenWorldsYA.com to sign up!

Prefer social media? All my links are listed under my bio, at the end of the book.

COLLECT ALL THE BOOKS IN THE SERIES

Don't miss out on a single step in Juliana's and Elisabeth's journeys. You can order the books below from your favourite book store or online retailer.

AVAILABLE IN REGULAR PRINT, LARGE PRINT, AND EBOOK

1. The Move
2. The Distance
3. The First Step
4. What Friends Do
5. Hide and Seek
6. Missing Home
7. What Will Come
8. A Father's Journey
9. The last book! Coming in 2024.

Also check out my blog for more background information about the series. You'll read about some of the research that went into the book, discover more about the real Canadian neighbourhoods used in the book, and learn about writing. Visit www.BetweenWorldsYA.com.

ACKNOWLEDGEMENTS

I'd like to thank the following people for their help with this book:

My mom, Gerda Wolf, and my dad, John Heffner, for not only enrolling me in dance but also for supporting my writing all these years, from pencil-and-paper to typewriter to computer.

My sister, Kristin Werner, for updating me with insights into the studio scene today.

Deardra King-Leslie, my tap and jazz teacher, for teaching me for over fifteen years and for tolerating all the times I was reading when I wasn't supposed to be.

Heather Wright, my consulting editor and writing coach, for advice on the early concept of the novel and the series.

Susan Fish of Storywell, my editor, who saw missed opportunities, wasted sentences, flattened characters, and more, and then helped me fix it all.

Jennifer Dinsmore, my proofreader, who finds the details that the rest of us can no longer see. (Any errors remaining are mine.)

Michelle Fairbanks of Fresh Design, my graphics designer, whose patience was greatly appreciated as we shuffled through dozens of photos to find the perfect ones for this cover.

ali macgee, who has unknowingly (unwittingly?) become my mentor.

Nick Tullius, for filling in a few details so I could make the second edition more accurate.

Tom Harding and Helena Calogeridis, librarians at the Dana Porter Library at the University of Waterloo, for helping me with my research and finding me an old encyclopedia I could actually use in the series. (A book that old feels electrical to a writer.)

The Heimatortsgemeinschaft Semlak and member Georg Schmidt for supplying me with much of the information I used to recreate Semlak in 1919.

The members of Donauschwaben Villages Helping Hands, who patiently answered many of my detailed questions about day-to-day life back then.

And finally, the Straus Haus: my husband Corey, and our two boys Khristopher and Jonnathan, who have supported my writing and had to deal with Mommy slipping away into her office every evening, and often on weekends, so she could finish the first book of a project she'd been dreaming of for years.

ABOUT THE 3RD EDITION

This is the third edition of *Between Worlds 1: The Move*. The second edition differed from the first edition in that it corrected some errors in historical facts, but changes to the third edition were much greater.

The Move first came out in 2018. It truly was a work from the heart, but I didn't know much about my writing style at the time or about the characters whose stories I was sharing. I had the energy and *inspiration* for the series; I was missing the *information* to breathe full life into its first book.

For example, in the first two editions, Juliana rarely interacted with her new family, and Elisabeth spent a good deal more time praying. Based on some reader feedback, this had two implications: Juliana appeared very self-entitled, and the religious content, though historically as correct as I could make it, was a little too much for some. I know some readers certainly enjoyed the first book! But I suspected many did not.

As I revised, I also found little touches where I could connect the chapters more for readers, such the differences in transportation (SUV vs. sleigh) and clothing (store-bought, brand-name winter clothing vs. handmade). I also chose to make clear that Juliana learned in the first book that the sketches belonged to an ancestor she'd been named after. Furthermore, the previous two editions didn't end with Juliana realizing she was holding another teenaged girl's art in her hands. I don't know how I missed that!

If you'd like to read the second edition for free to see which version you like better, it's available as an e-book to newsletter subscribers. Read the "Stay in Touch!" page for details.

Photo by Erin Watt Photography

Lori Wolf-Heffner is a former competitive dancer, dance teacher, and theatre manager. She was a member of the first Canadian National Tap Team, back in 1996, under the leadership of Bonnie Dyer, with choreographer Mathew Clark. She's written for *Dance Canada Quarterly, just dance!* magazine, and *The Dance Current* (all under Lori Straus).

Fluent in German, Lori lived in Germany for three years, never once realizing just how close she was to some of the villages her ancestors left to migrate to Eastern Europe in the 1700s.

Lori lives in Waterloo, Ontario, Canada, with her

husband and two sons. She is a member of The Writers'
Union of Canada and the Alliance of Independent
Authors.

facebook.com/loriwolfheffner
x.com/LoriWolfHeffner
instagram.com/loriwolfheffner
goodreads.com/lori_wolf-heffner
bookbub.com/author/lori-wolf-heffner
pinterest.com/loriwolfheffner
amazon.com/author/loriwolfheffner